SOUL'S DESIRE

Unparalleled Love Series

SHARON C. COOPER

ISBN: 978-1-946172-17-4
Paperback edition

Disclaimer

This story is a work of fiction. Names, characters, and incidents are either products of the author's imagination or are used fictitiously. Any resemblance to actual events, locales, organizations or persons, living or dead, is entirely coincidental.

Dear Reader,

I'm happy to announce that I, along with authors Stephanie Nicole Norris and Delaney Diamond, have collaborated to bring you a fun and sexy romance series! The *Unparalleled Love* series takes you on a journey of three friends who each find love and their happily-ever-after.

SOUL'S DESIRE is my contribution to the series and I can't wait until you meet Soul Carrington and Micah Olsen! They were college sweethearts and for reasons that you'll find out in the story, they went their separate ways. Don't worry, though, they do find their way back to each other, but not without a few challenges.

I hope you enjoy Soul and Micah's story as much as I enjoyed writing it!

For all of the fans of my *Atlanta's Finest* series, Soul Carrington is the little sister of Myles Carrington (think former CIA agent) who was introduced in ACCUSED (*Atlanta's Finest* series). **This story takes place at the same time as that story. Also, I'm happy to say that a couple of your favorite characters make guest appearances in this story!

Enjoy!

Sharon C. Cooper

NOTE: The Unparalleled Love Series can be read in any order.

Chapter One

ho says dreams don't come true?

Soul Carrington stood smiling inside the front entrance of the fifteen-hundred-square-foot building, excitement bubbling inside of her. The scent from freshly painted walls was lighter than it had been the day before, and the transformation was finally taking shape. Soft jazz flowed through the surround-sound speakers filling the space with a peace that she felt deep inside. She'd done it. She had finally accomplished one of her long-time goals—opening a dance studio.

Finally.

The dream morphed into a goal during her ten-year stint with an international dance troupe. Now there were moments she still couldn't believe it had come to fruition.

She moved further into the building, glancing into the oversized room to her right. Floor-to-ceiling mirrors covered every wall except one which was a window that looked out onto the strip mall's parking lot. The open space had shiny hardwood flooring, two barres—an upper and lower one for the students, as well as a couple of benches along one of the walls. The space could easily accommodate fifty dancers.

Moving down the long hallway, she passed the space where walls had been built to enclose two smaller dance rooms, a lounge area, a small galley kitchen, and her office. It was more space than Soul had planned for, but enough to grow into.

She had recently taken over ownership of the business, as well as the building lease, when the previous owners decided to retire. They operated the dance school for over twenty years, built up a sizable clientele, and had become a staple in the community. Now it was all hers, including some of the equipment.

"All mine," she squealed inside the smallest of the dance rooms. Excitement rushed through her veins as she did a series of pique turns, her back straight and arms rounded. She gazed up at the popcorn ceiling, wanting to scream to the world that she'd done it. "I'm doing this. I am really doing this."

The only thing...or person...missing from her special moment was her father. Her hero. The man who lost his wife while gaining a daughter. When Soul was old enough to understand that her mother had died giving birth to her, she hated herself. Hated the fact that because of her, her mother would never hold her daughter. Nor would she be able to teach her all the girly things that mothers taught their little girls. Soul had also hated that she would never know her mother.

But her dad had been everything a girl could ever hope for in a father. Loving. Kind. Generous. He treated her like a princess. Supported every interest she had, and never complained about driving her to gymnastics, ballet, or swim classes. While she'd been touring with the dance troupe, he had been the one to give her the idea of opening her own dance studio one day. He had also left start-up money in his will.

I miss you, Daddy. It's because of you that this dream is finally a reality.

"Okay, where are we putting everything?"

Soul startled, her hand flying to her chest at the sound of her brother's voice. "God, you scared me!" So caught up in her thoughts, she hadn't realized they'd started unloading the moving truck.

Myles narrowed his eyes, studying her as if she was up to something. The former CIA analyst, or so he liked everyone to believe, didn't miss much. Soul didn't have any proof, and he and their brother, Ray, who lived in Los Angeles, never confirmed it. But she was pretty sure Myles was once a CIA secret agent. It was in the way he processed information, the confident way he carried himself, and that air of mysteriousness that followed him around. He was also freakishly quiet when he moved, popping up out of nowhere at any given moment.

"You all right?" he asked, now standing in front of

her. He had been her rock for the past year after their father died, and then again when her fiancé suddenly decided he didn't want to get married. Myles helped Soul realize it was time to make some changes in her life. He showed up on her doorstep months ago, determined to move her back to Atlanta.

Why not, she'd thought. There had been nothing left for her in Houston. Soul had packed up her bags and headed to Atlanta. So far, it had been one of the best decisions she'd made in a long time. Currently, she was living with two of her best friends, and she was fulfilling one of her dreams.

"I'm fine," Soul finally answered, digging out a scrunchy from the front pocket of her denim shorts and pulling her hair into a ponytail. While they moved the furniture in, she'd start tackling some of the cleaning. The studio was re-opening in a week, and she wanted the place to look perfect for the grand opening.

"Okay, then. Show Laz and me where you want everything to go." At that moment, his friend and co-worker, Lazarus Dimas strolled into the room, his intense eyes doing a quick sweep of the space. Like her brother, he stood over six feet tall with broad shoulders and a badass vibe that bounced off of him in waves. He was also downright gorgeous with olive skin, hazel-green eyes that seemed to take everything in, and a bad-boy attitude that said, *yeah, I'm the shit so watch yourself.*

Soul had met him a little more than a year ago when

he was still a detective with Atlanta PD. Now, he worked with her brother as a security specialist for Supreme Security. Most referred to the specialists as *Atlanta's Finest*, providing personal security to some of the wealthiest people in the country. They stemmed from every branch of law enforcement. The few of them that Soul had met were definitely some badasses.

Laz removed the baseball cap he was wearing and ran his fingers through his dark hair that curled at his nape before replacing the hat. "This is a nice place, but you're going to need a new lock on the back door. One solid kick near the handle and the whole damn thing might fall apart."

"Yeah, I told her the same thing," Myles said. "I'll take care of it later. Now tell us where you want every-thing to go."

"Okay, the sofa, upholstered chairs, and the lamp go in this room," she said, leading them a short distance down the hallway to the lounge area that she was setting up for parents. Most of the classes would be an hour. She wanted them to have the option of sticking around in a comfortable setting while they waited for their children.

"The desk, leather chair, and file cabinet will go in the small room, the third door on the right." She had hoped to find a two-story building. That way her office could be in a separate part of the building, but she couldn't pass up the deal she'd gotten for the existing business.

An hour later, Soul wiped her sweaty forehead with her forearm. Even indoors with the air conditioner up high, summer heat in Atlanta was torturous.

"Hello? Anyone here?" a deep voice called out. A voice that Soul hadn't heard in over fifteen years. A voice that sent a wave of awareness crashing through her body, nipping at each nerve.

It can't be.

With her heart doing a little jig inside her chest, she quickly washed her hands in the bathroom sink, trying not to get her hopes up, but failing miserably. Since moving back to Atlanta, she had thought of him more often than not, but hadn't planned on seeking him out.

Taking a deep breath and releasing it slowly, Soul headed to the front of the building, her pulse pounding in her ears. Maybe she shouldn't be too excited to see him again, considering the way things had ended between them, but she couldn't help it.

Soul slowed when she spotted the man who would forever be ingrained in her heart. Micah Olsen. Her first love. Her only true love.

He and her brother shook hands, then pulled each other into a man-hug, pounding one another on the back. They fell into a deep conversation, talking like old friends. Sure, they'd met many years ago, but they seemed more familiar than she would've expected.

As if sensing her presence, they both turned.

Soul's breath stalled in her throat when her gaze

clashed with Micah's. Those whiskey-colored eyes bored into her, piercing her with a need she hadn't felt in ages, leaving her unable to move or speak. The years had indeed been good to him. Micah had always been gorgeous with his smooth, pecan-brown skin. But the man standing only ten feet from her now was mouthwatering *fine*!

In college, he wore his hair in cornrows, which Soul hated, and his face was always clean-shaven. Now he sported a low fade and a little scruff on his face, which she liked. Back then he was athletically built, like a basketball player. Now, his large frame had filled out in all the right places. His white T-shirt hugged his wide chest and broad shoulders, while his biceps bulged beneath the short sleeves.

A magnetic force surged through her body as his appreciative gaze slid over her from head to toe. Every nerve ending within her was standing at attention. How could he still have such an effect on her? It had been like forever since they'd seen each other.

Ugh. If only she had known he was coming. She would've gotten cleaned up instead of letting him see her all grungy and sweaty.

"Hey, beautiful." His deep voice settled around her, sending tingles swarming over her skin. "You're even prettier than I remember."

Ever since Myles called him a few days ago, needing a favor regarding Soul, Micah wondered what it would be like to see her again. But nothing could've prepared him for the stunning beauty in front of him. Those large expressive eyes held him captive until he allowed his gaze to take in the rest of the stunning package. He gave extra attention to the tank top that covered perky breasts and toned legs beneath the tiny denim shorts. He hadn't been kidding when he said she was prettier than he remembered.

Since she was rooted in place, looking as if she was holding her breath, Micah walked toward her. Only two steps in and she rushed toward him, leaping into his arms. His heart nearly burst out of his chest as she snuggled into him. Burying his face into the crook of her neck, Micah held her close, never wanting to let her go again. His eyes drifted closed as he soaked up her heady lavender scent and the softness of her body.

"Ms. Prissy…God, I've missed you," he said, placing a feathery kiss against her cheek before finally setting her back on her feet.

"What did I tell you about calling me that?" she said haughtily, her lips twitching to keep from smiling. Petite, prim, and proper, she might've hated the nickname, but the name fit her perfectly.

Micah held her hand and stood back to get another look at her. It had been years since he'd seen Soul. When they dated, he'd always wanted to feed her, put some meat on her bones, but dancing was her life. Maintaining her slim figure was her top priority. Since then, she had filled out a little, adding some nice curves to her lithe body.

Micah's gaze went back to her face, her smooth, dark skin glistening from the humidity. She was one of those women who didn't need makeup. Her natural beauty shined through, and those lips... Lord, those sweet pouty lips that he used to feast on all those years ago were still as tempting as they'd been back then.

"It's so good to see you," she said just above a whisper, staring as if she couldn't believe he was standing there.

"Likewise, baby." Unable to help himself, Micah pulled her back into his arms, holding her tight. His biggest regret was walking out of her life, and there'd been too many days that he longed to have her in his arms again.

"You know what? That's enough of this shit. I get it. You both are happy to see each other," Myles ground out, irritation in his tone as he frowned at Micah. "Let her go and back the hell up."

Micah loosened his hold and laughed. "Man, you don't scare me anymore. Besides, she's grown now."

"Oh please. I was grown then. He just always treated me like a kid."

Myles shrugged. "You'll always be my kid sister. I couldn't let punks like him push up on you without laying down the law."

"Yeah, he definitely laid down the law," Micah

grinned, shaking his head as memories of that first meeting came to mind. "I'll never forget the first day I met Myles. I was on my way home from playing basketball at the rec center, and your brother comes out of nowhere. Like a damn ninja ghost, he materialized out of thin air. Scared the crap out of me."

Soul laughed while Myles smirked.

"I remember you telling me about that night," Soul said, smiling before glancing at her brother. "What I don't remember is how you found out he and I were dating."

"I have my ways," Myles said without elaborating.

Micah's mind drifted back to that night in the alley. He wasn't easily intimidated, but there was something about Myles that would spook the bravest man. Myles was a few years older and now the two of them were close in height, but Micah was about ten or fifteen pounds heavier. In college, Soul had mentioned her brothers, but at that time, he hadn't met either of them.

Being the only girl and the baby of the family, her brothers and father had been fiercely protective of her. Micah had later learned that her mother died during childbirth. Considering how Myles had hunted him down back then, and again recently to ask Micah for a favor, Soul probably had no clue the lengths her brother would go to protect her.

"Now yo' ass shows up after we've unloaded the truck," Laz said to Micah as he strolled from the back of the building.

"Ahh, man. Y'all just let anybody up in here," Micah cracked, laughing as he stuck his hand out to Laz, and they pulled each other into a hug. "Long time no see, man. What's going on? And what's this crazy rumor I've been hearing about you being married to the assistant district attorney, *and* with a baby on the way?"

Laz chuckled. "Those are facts, son. It was time."

"Besides, he had to marry her. He needs someone close by to keep his ass out of jail," Myles added.

"Don't even go there. Now I know it's time to go before they put all my business out here."

Soul turned to Micah. "How do you know Laz?"

"Micah's a cop," Laz volunteered before Micah could respond.

Soul's brows shot up. "Really?" she said. With that one word, Micah couldn't tell if that was only surprise in her tone, or surprise with a hint of disapproval.

After his last tour with the Marine Corps, he had joined Atlanta PD, following in his father, grandfather, and great-grandfather's footsteps. He had met Laz a few years ago and liked him immediately. He was no-nonsense and had earned a reputation of being a by-any-means-necessary kind of cop to get bad guys off the streets. The man didn't play.

"Well, we gotta get going. We'll leave you two to catch up," Myles said, strolling over to Soul, then kissed her on the cheek. "Call me if you want anything else moved. Better yet, get muscle man over there," he said, pointing at Micah, "to take care of it. I'll be back later to change out the backdoor lock."

Once they were gone, Soul said, "So, you're a cop. What else don't I know about you?"

"Have dinner with me tonight, and I'll tell you anything you want to know."

Chapter Two

*S*oul burst through the front door of the house, only having forty minutes to get cleaned up and changed before Micah picked her up for dinner.

"Anyone home?" she called out while walking farther into the large four-bedroom, four-bathroom home she shared with her best friends. She glanced in the office, then the dining room before heading to the back of the house.

Jada, who had inherited the home from her grandfather, insisted Soul move in with her and Janice. That idea had been a godsend, giving Soul a chance to save some money and open her dance studio sooner than expected. The three of them living together might've been temporary, but she loved having her friends to come home to.

It didn't hurt that the house was absolutely gorgeous. Bright and airy with floor-to-ceiling windows, thanks to a recent remodel. Jada, an interior designer, had turned the home into a masterpiece. Pearl white covered most of the walls with a few accent walls sprinkled throughout the home. Bold pops of color accents and furniture made the place look like something straight out of *House Beautiful* magazine.

"Jan? Jada? You guys home?"

Soul hurried down the hall toward the kitchen and practically ran into Jada. "Oh, hey. I was starting to think no one was here." Based on the fitted T-shirt, yoga pants, and her hair in a loose ponytail on top of her head, it was safe to say Jada had just returned from the gym. She was the only person Soul knew who was always in full makeup wherever she went. Even after a hard workout, the woman still looked fabulous.

"I was finishing up a call with a client." She looked Soul up and down. "What's up? You look like you're about to burst from excitement."

"You're never going to believe who came to the studio today," Soul said, giddiness swirling inside of her as she grabbed a bottle of water from the oversize refrigerator. The state-of-the-art kitchen was a cook's paradise with stainless steel appliances, stone countertops, and a wall of windows that looked out over the deck and picturesque backyard.

"Who came to the studio today?"

Soul turned at the sound of Janice's voice as she strolled into the kitchen, carrying an armful of grocery bags. Her long, curly hair was pulled back with a headband, and her face glistened with a light sheen of perspiration. It had been so hot in Atlanta the last few days that Soul had found herself sweating while standing still.

"Sooo, what did I miss?" Janice asked.

"Actually, you're right on time. I was just getting ready to tell Jada who I saw today." Soul started unpacking one of the bags, putting carrots and swiss cheese into the refrigerator. She was still reeling at seeing Micah again. "Guess who I was just with?"

"Who?" they both yelled, and Soul laughed.

"Quit messing around and just tell us," Janice grumbled, storing items in the pantry.

"Micah Olsen."

"Okay, now you have my attention. When? Where? And how?" Janice asked.

"Forget all of that. How'd he look?" Jada asked. "Does he still wear his hair in braids?"

Soul shook her head. "Girl, nah. Thank God. The man is absolutely beautiful." She told them about the furniture being moved and how Micah showed up looking absolutely delicious. For the next few minutes they lobbed questions at her, and Soul realized just how much she didn't know about him.

"Hopefully, I'll find all of that out when we get together."

"Was it awkward seeing him again, considering how you guys just suddenly broke up?" Janice studied her, a curious glint radiating in her eyes.

Soul had never told them the real reason why she and

Micah parted ways, but she always wondered if they somehow knew. If they did, neither ever said anything.

"No, it wasn't awkward. I have never been so happy to see someone in my life. You know how I felt about him. All the old feelings from before rushed back and…" she shrugged, not knowing what else to say.

"Are you ever going to tell us what happened between you two?" Jada asked, her voice gentle as if knowing the pain Soul had felt back then had also returned to the forefront.

"I told you. We wanted different things." Wanting and needing to end the direction that the conversation was going, Soul glanced at the thin watch on her arm. "I need to hurry up. He'll be here soon."

Was it awkward seeing him again?

Janice's words rattled through Soul's mind as anxiousness clawed through her body while she jogged up the stairs to the second floor. Thankfully, seeing Micah again hadn't been awkward, but she'd hated the way things ended between them. Neither of them wanted to break up, but it had been for the best.

Soul stood inside her walk-in closet, debating on what to wear to dinner. No matter how cool she'd tried to be when Micah invited her out, she had been caught off guard. It had already been a shock to her system, seeing him after so many years. Now they were planning to share a meal.

"Maybe I should've said no," she mumbled to herself. All the old lustful feelings she'd always felt whenever he was near had bombarded her immediately. It never failed. He stirred something so passionate within her; even now, it was easy to forget that they were just friends. At least they used to be. If his more-than-friends greeting was any indication, there were no hard feelings between them. But how was she going to sit across from him for any length of time without drooling over the man?

She shivered and smiled, recalling how mouthwatering gorgeous he was. She would've been a fool to turn down dinner and miss being in his presence, if for nothing more than to stare at his handsome face. Any awkwardness would be worth it.

Soul reached for the white floral sundress that stopped just above her knees and a pair of strappy white sandals. The form-fitting outfit always made her feel feminine, yet bold and in control. If she were a mess inside, at least she'd look cute on the outside.

She hurried and slipped out of her robe and lotioned her body before sliding into a lacy bra and panty set. It had been ages since she'd been on a date.

"Wait. This is not a date," she reminded herself. They were just two people going to hang out. She hadn't been out with a man since before Ryan.

A twinge of discomfort pierced her chest. Just thinking about her ex-fiancé sparked a riot of emotions, anger, disappointment, and confusion being amongst them. How could he have broken off their engagement without warning and then disappear?

Ryan had moved out of his apartment, changed his

cell phone number, and had taken some of the cash out of their joint account and *poof*. He was gone. At least he had left enough money to cover all of the wedding debt, as well as enough for her to live on for a couple of months. But it was the way the whole situation played out that confused her.

Soul knew now that she wasn't in love with Ryan, but at the time, she thought he could provide what she really desired. A loving relationship. Still, he walked away without looking back.

A knock sounded on her door just as she zipped her dress.

"Come in." Soul sat on the edge of the bed to slip on her sandals.

Jada strolled in with a goofy grin on her face. She had changed into an oversized sleeveless Clark Atlanta University shirt, skinny jeans and a pair of flip-flops. Soul was pretty sure the shirt belonged to Solomon, Jada's best friend from childhood, but she didn't say anything.

"Your *date* is here. And can I just say, your description of him didn't do him justice. He almost doesn't look like the same guy from years ago. That's a grown-ass man down there, girl!"

All Soul could do was smile when her friend started fanning herself. From the moment they all spotted Micah across the pizza joint near Spelman, they'd all agreed that he was a cutie.

"I second that, but that grown-ass man is fifteen

minutes early. I barely had enough time to take a shower."

"Yeah, he said he was a little early and for me to not rush you. So, where's he taking you?"

Soul hurried into the bathroom to put on mascara and lip gloss. "I'm not sure, but I'm surprised you didn't give him the third degree."

Jada stood in the bathroom doorway, that stupid grin back on her face. "I left Janice to handle that. You know how good she is at questioning folks."

Yes, Soul did know. Their friend really should've been a lawyer. Instead, she worked in finance for a hotel chain.

"Are you taking an overnight bag?" Jada wiggled her eyebrows suggestively.

"Uh, *no*. We're just going out to catch up on each other's lives. Nothing else. This isn't a date or a reunion." At least that's what Soul kept telling herself.

"Mmm-hmm. We'll see. Remember, I was there when you guys fell for each other. Had it been left up to Micah, you two would've been married within weeks of meeting."

True. Even if her friend was right, Soul wasn't ready to go there. Otherwise, she'd have to come clean about why they broke up in the first place.

"Enough about me," Soul said after one last look in the mirror. She turned to her friend. It was good to see Jada's easygoing side shining through. Lately, she'd been a little down, going through a rough patch with her boyfriend. "How are you?"

Jada's shoulders drooped, and she rubbed the back of her neck. "I'm all right. Just...I just have a lot on my mind. I need to make some serious decisions, and I'm still trying to decide on which direction to take."

Soul hoped those decisions included Solomon—Jada's longtime friend who was one of the nicest guys Soul knew. If only Jada could see how much he adored her and not just in a *friend* kind of way. The man would walk across a shark-infested ocean for the woman.

"Let's table this conversation for another day," Jada said. "Try to have fun tonight, and if you do decide to stay out all night, shoot one of us a text, so we'll know you're okay."

Soul nodded. She wanted to ask more questions but instead let it go. Jada would talk when she was ready.

Soul took one last look in the mirror and ran her fingers through her loose curls that hung around her shoulders. Usually, she wore her hair up with a few strands hanging in her face to cover what she felt was a large forehead. Tonight, she had decided to wear it down.

"How do I look?" She slowly turned around in a circle with her arms out so that her friend could give her opinion on the outfit as a whole.

"Like you have to ask. You look as beautiful as usual. Heck, with that body you could make a potato sack look hot. I love the dress, but you better watch yourself. Micah won't be able to keep his hands off of you in that sexy little number."

Soul laughed. "Thanks, girl. I'm crazy nervous. I haven't seen him in so long, and don't even get me started on how long it's been since I've been on a date."

"So, it is a date?"

Oh crap.

"No," Soul said quickly over her friend's laughter. "It's not a date. We're just catching up with each other."

"Yeah, sure. Tell it to someone who doesn't know better. More than that, tell it to someone who doesn't know how much in love you two used to be."

Instead of responding, Soul grabbed her small handbag, checking to make sure she had her cell phone and house keys. She followed Jada out of the room and to the stairs, trying to tamp down her anxiousness.

It's only Micah. Nothing to be nervous about.

That thought died when she made it to the bottom step and saw him. Butterflies took flight in her gut, and her mouth went dry. *Goodness.* The man had a visceral effect on her that Soul couldn't deny. She still couldn't get over how huge he was. The light blue polo shirt stretched across his wide, muscular chest, revealing just how fit he was. Her gaze went lower to the dark pants that covered powerful thighs and long legs.

"Hey," he said, smiling, his gaze taking in her attire before returning to her face. "You look amazing."

"You do, too," she said, sounding like a high-schooler heading out on a first date.

"So, where are you kids going?" Jada asked, her arms

folded across her chest as she and Janice stood nearby like mother hens.

Micah started to respond, but Soul stopped him with a hand on his arm. "Don't answer that. They're just being nosy. Besides, I'm sure Janice has already asked you more than enough questions. Bye, ladies." Soul ushered him to the door. "Don't wait up."

"Amongst other things, I can't wait to find out how the three of you ended up rooming together again," Micah said, holding the door open.

"Yeah, I guess we have a lot to discuss."

Micah sat across from Soul. The dim bulb in the light fixture over the table had barely offered sufficient light to read the menu a few minutes ago. Still, it illuminated just enough brightness to accentuate Soul's loveliness and the gentle smile gracing her pretty lips.

"This is a nice place. I've driven by here a few times, and it's bigger than I thought inside," she said, her gaze steady on him.

When Micah chose the cozy restaurant, he had mainly selected it because of the diverse menu. He hadn't necessarily tried to pick a romantic place, but that's precisely what he'd done. Hushed conversations flowed around them and light contemporary music playing in the background only added to the relaxed atmosphere. But despite the calming environment, Soul was still fidgeting.

"I'm sorry if I keep staring at you," she said, diverting her eyes as she nervously picked at some imaginary lint on the white tablecloth. "It's just that it's a little weird seeing you again."

Micah reached out and covered her hand with his, and like each other time he had touched her tonight, a jolt of energy shot through him. It had been a long time since a woman affected him like this. "Relax," he told her, squeezing her hand before slowly releasing it. "I know exactly how you feel. When I stopped by your dance studio, I wasn't sure how you would respond."

Deciding to break up in college had been a mutual agreement. At least Micah felt it was mutual since it had been clear they hadn't wanted the same thing for their future. The last thing he had wanted to do was walk away from what they had, but he'd done it to protect himself. Whether she knew it or not, Soul had owned his heart and had the ability to hurt him like no other. He couldn't let that happen.

"Sitting across from you like this is surreal. What's it been, fourteen, fifteen years?" Micah asked.

"Well, I graduated from college fourteen years ago, and you left in my sophomore year. That means it's been sixteen years since I've seen you."

Micah lowered his gaze to the beer glass, his finger sliding up the side of it, catching some of the condensation.

If he had to do his life over again, he'd start with his last few months at Morehouse College. Leaving after his sophomore year to join the Marine Corps had served two purposes—get away from Soul and find another way to pay for college.

Leaving had seemed like a good idea at the time. His and Soul's desires weren't aligned, which sparked his initial thoughts about leaving town. As for paying for college, without a scholarship, tuition proved impossible to pay out of pocket. When the meager paychecks he was getting from his part-time house-painting job didn't put a dent in the cost, he knew he had to go a different route.

"All right, here we go," the server said. "I have the ginger teriyaki stir-fry for you." She set the sizeable steaming dish in front of Soul, "And the prime rib, potatoes, and vegetables for you. Can I get either of you anything else?"

"No. This looks great," Soul said.

"How about you? Would you like another beer?" the server asked, nodding toward Micah's half-empty beer glass.

He shook his head. "No, thanks, but could I get a glass of water?" He was off duty but had picked up an early morning shift. The last thing he needed to do was indulge in one too many beers.

"Sure, I'll be right back with that."

Before he could start digging into his meal, the server returned, setting two glasses of water on the table. As they ate, small talk about the weather, traffic, and Soul's roommates flowed easily which didn't surprise Micah.

They'd been friends before they officially started dating and had never had a problem communicating.

"Tell me what you've been up to since the last time I saw you," Soul said, now picking at her food. Micah didn't know how she survived. Even when they were dating, she ate like a bird.

"Well, as you know, I joined the Marine Corps after leaving Morehouse. I did eventually get my degree in criminal justice."

"That's great. I wondered if you ever went back to school. I know a few people who took a break from college and never returned. Was it difficult to take classes while serving?"

For the next few minutes, Micah shared stories about his military life. It had been hard juggling serving and taking classes. Some he did online, while other times he attended night school when his schedule allowed. But not getting his degree wasn't an option. Graduating college had been instilled in him as a kid, especially since his father barely had a high school diploma.

"What was it like for you in the military? Did you have to go overseas?"

Micah nodded. He rarely discussed his time in the military, not wanting to drum up memories that he'd tried to forget. Especially the ones where he'd lost friends, friends who were closer than brothers. Though he had sustained a few non-life-threatening injuries while serving, too many of his brothers in arms couldn't say the same—some of the things Micah had experienced and witnessed while overseas would forever be burned into his memory.

"Yeah. I did a couple of tours in Afghanistan and Iraq, and spent time in Alaska, Africa, and Japan."

Soul nodded as she studied him, her gorgeous eyes searching his. Micah wasn't sure what she was looking for or if she sensed this was a subject he really didn't want to discuss. Either way, she didn't ask him to expound. They ate in companionable silence.

"I also got married a few years after joining the military," he said between bites.

Soul's fork stopped mid-air, her mouth gaping as she slowly lowered the utensil to her dish. "You're married?" she croaked before clearing her throat, her eyes big and her back straight. Like a switch had been turned on, Micah could already see her putting up invisible walls around herself.

"I *was*," he hurried to say. "She was killed eight years ago at a women's shelter she'd been volunteering at."

Soul gasped, her hand going to her mouth. "Oh, my goodness. Micah, I am so sorry for your loss."

Micah sucked in a breath and released it slowly as he glanced around the now-crowded restaurant, trying to steady the erratic beat of his heart. It had been a long time ago, but now and then he allowed himself to remember one of the darkest times in his life. He had mourned his wife's death and dealt with the guilt that had practically eaten him up. But that didn't stop those old feelings from creeping back in.

He cut a piece of steak and put it into his mouth, trying not to let regrets get the best of him. Brooklyn had been one of the nicest women he'd ever met, and he loved her in his own special way. Unfortunately, he hadn't loved her enough—not the way a husband should love his wife.

"Tell me what happened," Soul said softly.

As much as Micah loved steak, suddenly the tender meat tasted like cardboard on his tongue as memories crept through his mind. Maybe he shouldn't have mentioned Brooklyn, but it would've been hard to tell Soul what he'd been up to over the years without mentioning his late wife.

He set his fork down and took a long swig of his beer before responding. In hindsight, maybe he should've had the server bring him another one.

"The estranged husband of one of the residents at the shelter hunted his wife down there. He ended up killing her, a staff person, and Brooklyn, my wife. I was overseas when it happened."

Guilt like nothing he had ever experienced before had eaten Micah up that first year. Brooklyn had asked him more than once to leave the military, come home, and find a job. She hated the distance, and she'd wanted them to start a family but not while he was still serving. She hadn't wanted to raise their children by herself, and Micah agreed. He had always wanted a big family. And while he might've loved his wife, would've done anything for her, there had always been something missing in their relationship. They hadn't had that I-can't-live-without-you type of love, but he'd had every intention of upholding his vows. Despite those issues, he had wanted the relationship to work, but then she was gone.

Soul covered his hand with her smaller one and squeezed. "You had to be devastated."

Micah nodded. He had been but probably not for the reasons she was thinking. Regret had eaten at him from the inside out for not being there for her, for not being able to love her the way he wanted to. He hadn't been able to be the man she needed and deserved.

After the attack, by the time he had arrived stateside, she had died. He told Soul about those months that followed. Not about how awful he felt by his inability to truly love his wife, but how angry he had been for not being home. He was out protecting his country but hadn't been able to protect his wife.

"I know how much you wanted to get married and have a family," Soul said quietly, pulling her hand away. Micah immediately felt the loss of her gentle touch. "I am so sorry you went through that. Did you two have any children?"

Micah shook his head. "We were planning to start a family once I left the military, but I kept putting it off."

Since he didn't have any siblings, he had always wanted a large family, but it never seemed to be the right time. Or at least that's what he let himself believe. Now, getting married and having children occupied much of his thoughts. At thirty-six, he wasn't getting any younger and didn't want to be too old to chase after his kids. Though his desire to have children hadn't waned, until recently, he hadn't been interested in having a long-term relationship. He didn't think he'd ever be able to find a woman who made him want to open his heart completely again.

"Okay, enough about me," he said, getting uncomfortable in the way his thoughts were going. "Tell me about you. Oh, but for the record. You might not have seen me since college, but I've seen you."

Her brows shot up. "Really? When? Where? And why didn't you say something?"

"London. Five years ago. The dance troupe you were touring with had a few shows there. I attended one of them and heard that you had choreographed part of it."

"Oh, Micah. I wish I had known you were there. It would've been good to see you."

He had wanted to talk to her, let her know he was there, but thought better of it. His mother was the only person who knew that he had never honestly gotten over Soul. It wasn't because he'd told her. Somehow, she had guessed and told him to either reach out to Soul or move on.

That night in London, seeing his favorite ballerina on stage looking like an angel, he had considered his mother's words. For years he had tried burying his feelings for Soul, but she was never far from his mind. A couple of years into his marriage, and especially when he kept postponing leaving the military, Brooklyn had asked if there was someone else. He assured her that he would never, ever cheat on her, but thoughts of Soul had often invaded his mind.

"The show was phenomenal; I shouldn't have been surprised. You've always been an amazing dancer, and your skills, strength, and moves that night had me spellbound."

"How close were you sitting?"

"Second row, center stage."

A huge smile spread across her lips. It was all he could do to stop himself from reaching over and capturing her mouth with his.

Yep, it was good he hadn't sought her out while in London. That would've been a colossal mistake. Seeing her that night had stirred something fierce inside of him. And sitting across from her now had him wanting to pick up where they'd left off while in college.

But he knew better.

They didn't want the same things out of life back in the day, and he was pretty sure that hadn't changed.

"I was surprised to hear that you were no longer touring."

The smile slowly slipped from Soul's face, and she nodded. "I sprained my ankle shortly after that last show in London. After recovering, I suffered another injury, and then another one. Each injury took longer to recover from, and when I got hip bursitis, I took that as a sign. It was time to hang up my ballet shoes."

"I'm sorry to hear that. For as long as I've known you, all you've ever wanted to do was dance."

Which was partly why they had broken up. She lived and breathed dancing, and though Micah knew she had loved him as much as he loved her, she hadn't wanted marriage and kids. He knew then that they could never have a life together.

"That's true, but touring the world is in the past. Now I'm focused on getting my business off the ground."

Micah bit the inside of his cheek, trying to keep from asking what he really wanted to know. Bitterness wasn't a good taste but damned if he wasn't still a little resentful.

"Tell me something, Soul. How the hell could you agree to marry someone when you told me that you would never get married?"

Chapter Three

*S*tunned by the bite behind Micah's words, Soul sat back in her seat. She didn't miss the hurt in his eyes and felt just as bad as she had when they broke up. Shame settled inside of her, picking at the scab that covered a portion of her heart. The part that barely healed when Micah walked out of her life.

He had a right to be a little angry. She had told him that she would *never* get married. Yet, the first person to come along after him and propose, she'd said yes.

"His name was Ryan Frasier. I met him shortly after I stopped touring. We dated a couple of months, and then he proposed."

She went back to eating, needing something to do to keep from seeing the pain in Micah's eyes. Shoveling the stir fry and rice into her mouth, she barely tasted the food. How did their nice, comfortable evening suddenly go off track?

Soul glanced up when Micah sat back and folded his thick arms across his massive chest. His gaze bore into her like a laser beam finding its target.

"I'm surprised you said yes. You told me that you could never make that type of commitment. That you never wanted to settle down. What happened to you not wanting to get married...*ever?*"

"Micah, that was a long time ago. I was young and naïve. People change. *I* changed."

She set her fork down, needing him to understand that she wasn't that same narrow-minded girl. She wanted him to know that just because she hadn't wanted marriage and a family back then, that wasn't the case now. Her biggest fear was growing old alone with no one to love and no one to love her.

Yes, she'd said that she didn't ever want anything to do with marriage. And kids had been out of the question since her mother had died during childbirth. Despite her father telling her that she shouldn't rule out kids because of fear of dying, she had. But now...

"I've changed, Micah. My needs and desires are very different than they were in college. I want marriage," she said but stopped short of saying she wanted children. Deep down, she would love to have two kids, and some days she thought she was ready. But the fear of dying during childbirth was real, almost crippling. Her heart still ached for the mother she never knew. The mother who basically gave her life so that Soul could live.

No. I'm not going to think about that right now. Right now,

Soul needed Micah to know that she wasn't the same person she'd been back in college. That she wanted what most women wanted. A love of a lifetime. A family to call her own.

"When you left school and joined the Marines, I thought my heart would never heal. I barely got through the next two years of school, and then the opportunity to tour with the troupe came along."

Soul released a long sigh. Those days seemed like a lifetime ago.

"I realized soon after I started my career that I wanted more. I needed more. Even with thirty other people around me every day, all day, it was a lonely life, Micah."

He ran his hand over his mouth. "I know that feeling."

"But with our tour schedule, practicing, traveling, performing…there wasn't time to meet someone and build an intimate relationship." She had thought of Micah often, wondering where he was, how he was doing, and what he was up to. "Honestly, I thought I had missed my opportunity to have a special love."

Micah huffed out a breath. "Then you met Ryan and fell in love."

Soul gave a slight shrug. "I thought I had, but…" Embarrassment coursed through her veins. How could she tell him that she was going to marry a guy that she didn't really and truly love?

Something must be wrong with me, she thought. Ryan had always been sweet, kind, and caring. He was handsome, made good money as an accountant, and he made her feel special. He wanted to spend the rest of his life with her.

At least that's what he'd led her to believe.

Micah sat forward and moved his plate to the side. He folded his forearms on the table. "But what? Are you saying that you didn't love him?"

She met his gaze. Staring into his gorgeous, intense, whiskey-brown eyes, Soul wondered how she could've been so careless in letting him walk away. They'd been perfect together. He had been perfect...perfect for her. If only they had wanted the same thing at the time.

"I thought I loved him," she finally said. "When he called and told me that he couldn't marry me, that we had to call off the wedding, I was pissed. Confused. Hurt. I was angry enough to slash his tires, but I didn't know where he was."

"Well, I guess that's good."

Soul rolled her eyes and smiled. "Yeah, you're probably right. The last thing I needed was to end up in jail. Anyway, I don't think I stayed mad long enough."

His brows dipped into a frown. "What do you mean?"

"I mean he broke my heart and I was ticked the hell off for a while, but then..." She shook her head. "I wasn't. I don't miss him. I only think about him every now and then. While it took me at least ten years to get over you, with him, it took me a month. Now when I think about him, all I do is call him horrible names for dumping me and for disappearing."

"So, he disappeared? You haven't seen him, talked to him…no type of contact with him?"

She shook her head, anger creeping up inside her chest. "Not a word. It's like I meant nothing to him. Like he forgot I even existed."

"I doubt that's the case. You're unforgettable."

Soul sat stunned by his words. Micah finished off his beer, acting as if he hadn't just said words she needed to hear. Words that made her heart sing.

He set the beer glass down with a *thunk*. "The stupid bastard was a fucking asshole."

Her mouth dropped open. He said the words with so much conviction. It was as if he actually knew Ryan. Either way, his words were accurate.

Unable to help herself, she burst out laughing. She cackled even harder when Micah looked at her as if she had lost her mind. Back in college, Soul could count on one hand the number of times she'd heard him curse. Micah wasn't that guy. Besides her father, he was the most patient, easy-going, and tolerant person she'd ever known. Those who knew him, loved him, and vice versa. Hearing the vehement disgust in his tone when referring to Ryan was too funny.

"Thank you for that," Soul said, dabbing at the tears in the corner of her eyes with the cloth napkin.

"For what?" he asked, confusion covering his handsome face.

Soul could kiss him. Really kiss him. But she wouldn't. She couldn't. They weren't together, probably would never be able to pick up where they'd left off. Besides, one kiss would never be enough. He'd be an addiction she'd never want to beat.

"Why are you thanking me, Soul?"

"For the laugh. For saying what you did." There'd been a time when she wouldn't have thought sweet kind Ryan could just walk away without an explanation.

"Maybe you saying yes to the asshole's marriage proposal is more about you not wanting to marry me."

Whoa. Wait. "What?" Now Soul was looking at him as if he was the one who was crazy. "That doesn't even make sense. I have never loved another man the way I loved you, but that's beside the point, Micah. I haven't seen you in like…forever."

"And whose fault is that?" he said with force, causing people at a nearby table to look at them. He leaned forward and lowered his voice. "Your brother is former CIA. He can find anyone, anywhere, at any time. If you wanted to find me, all you had to do was ask him."

She had thought about doing just that on more than one occasion, but didn't tell Micah that. "What difference would it have made? You were already married."

"But you didn't know that," he spat, his jaw clenched, revealing a side of him that she'd never seen before.

Who is this man? And what happened to the gentle giant who she had fallen in love with in college?

"It wouldn't have mattered," Soul said dismissively.

"It *would have* mattered," Micah countered, then looked away, but not before she saw the hurt in his eyes. He pinched the bridge of his nose, then cursed under his breath.

It would have mattered. His words played on a loop inside her head as she continued studying him. Soul wasn't even sure what to say to that or anything that had just transpired in the last five minutes. Not once had Micah tried reaching out to her. Not after he joined the military. Not even after he claimed to see her in London. Never in a million years would she have thought he still had feelings for her.

That was if she understood him correctly.

A weighted silence fell between them. Soul wanted to ask more questions and even had a few that she'd like answered about his late wife. But the thought of talking about a woman who'd once had the life and the man that Soul wanted, didn't seem like a good idea.

She gathered her small purse and slipped the strap onto her shoulder. "Maybe we should go."

Micah ran his hands down his face and released a frustrated growl. "No. Baby...I mean...I'm sorry. That..." He waved his large hands back and forth as if trying to find words. "I was way out of line. I guess for years I thought somehow you and I would magically find our way back to each other."

"But, Micah, you were *married*," she whispered.

"I know. I know, but…"

"But?" Soul sat confused, trying to understand how he thought they'd ever find their way back to each other while he was married. He might not be the same man he'd been when he left for the military, but there was no way he had changed that much. There was no way she'd ever believe him to be a guy that would cheat on his wife. Ever.

"I never stopped loving you."

Soul's heart did a backflip inside her chest. "S—say what now?"

Heat rushed through her body as his penetrating gaze bore deep into her, sending her mind reeling in shock. How was it possible that he had never stopped loving her? Soul couldn't wrap her brain around how he'd been able to marry someone, even planned to start a family with the woman, yet claimed to have never stopped loving her.

"I—I—I don't know what to say," she stuttered.

You can't say anything since you almost married a man you didn't truly love, her traitorous brain taunted.

Micah removed a wad of money from his wallet and left it on the table before standing. He reached for her hand. "Let's get out of here."

Instead of insisting that he explain himself, Soul slipped her hand into his larger one and let him lead her out of the restaurant. Micah always had—and he always would—own a part of her heart, but could they ever have what they once had? Was that what his little outburst was about? Was that what he wanted? Heck, was that what she wanted?

This is crazy.

Chapter Four

I'm an idiot.

That was the only explanation Micah could come up with for why he hadn't kept his big mouth shut. As he guided Soul out of the restaurant, the comments he'd made at the table played around in his mind. It was one thing to fantasize about her, and even imagine what it would be like to have her as his again.

But it was a whole other beast to actually tell her that he had never stopped loving her.

The only highlight of the last few minutes was that he still had hold of her hand. If she was mad at his behavior, there was no way she'd let him touch her. Lucky for him, Soul wasn't confrontational and didn't like drama. She wasn't one to make a scene, especially out in public. Micah could count on one hand, with fingers left over, the number of times they actually argued about anything.

They made their way across the well-lit parking lot, skirting around parked cars until they arrived at Micah's truck. He unlocked the vehicle and opened the passenger side door, but when he lifted Soul's hand to help her into the tall vehicle, she pulled back.

Micah glanced down at her but didn't speak, figuring she'd say what was on her mind. He just hoped he hadn't totally blown things tonight.

Soul bit her lower lip, something she used to do often whenever nervous or unsure about something. Seconds ticked by as she glanced around their surroundings, looking at everything but him.

"Just say what you need to say," Micah prompted.

"When I told you I didn't want to get married and have children, I didn't know you were going to leave me. I was devastated. It was like having my heart ripped out of my chest, and for the record, there's still a void there that has never been filled. Just because I didn't want a family didn't mean that I didn't want to be with you. I honestly thought our love was strong enough to get us through anything."

Micah shook his head. "Soul…baby, I couldn't stay. For me, love and marriage go hand in hand. I don't think you understood just how much in love I was with you. I envisioned us spending the rest of our lives together. I knew how you felt about not having children, but even knowing that, I wanted you to one day be my wife. I wanted you to spend the rest of your life with me."

"Then you should've fought for me!" she snapped, shoving against his chest.

Her words crackled in the night with a potent bite that Micah wasn't used to hearing from her, and damn if they didn't stir something erotic within him.

"Like you said," she continued with the same no-nonsense tone, "I could've found you, but you could've found me, too. As a matter of fact, you did. You just chose not to make your presence known after the show in London. So, if you're mad or disappointed at anyone, be disappointed in yourself. Not me."

Micah shoved his hands into the front pockets of his dress pants. He didn't have a comeback. He couldn't say anything. She was right. He could've stayed in Atlanta, found a way to pay for college, and hoped she'd change her mind about them. But at the time, he didn't see that ever happening. Seeing her in London was a similar case. Why set himself up only to have her turn him down again?

At least he had been able to keep up with her over the years, thanks to Myles. If her brother knew that Micah was still crazy in love with Soul, he hadn't called him out on it. Yet, Myles freely provided answers whenever Micah inquired about her.

She might've admitted at dinner that she was ready to meet someone and get married, but that didn't mean that she wanted that someone to be Micah. It wasn't until he'd heard about Ryan, the broken engagement, and then the disturbing news about the man's extracurricular activities did Micah entertain the idea of having her back in his life. It's too bad he couldn't actually tell her that—at least not yet.

"I'm sorry," he said, "for everything. Clearly, I didn't do a good job in how I handled our situation back then, or with what I said tonight. You're important to me, Soul, and you always will be."

"I feel the same about you, but you need to understand something. I'm not the same person I was in college. My goals and desires are very different than they used to be."

Part of Micah wanted to ask her to elaborate, but he was a firm believer that one should never ask a question unless they are prepared for the answer. And right now, he was a little too emotionally wound up to guarantee a proper response to whatever she might say.

After finally helping her into the truck, Micah walked around the back of the vehicle and climbed into the driver's seat. He might not be ready to hear more about how she'd changed, but he also wasn't prepared for the evening to end. He drove in the opposite direction of Soul's house. If she noticed he was taking the scenic route to her place, she didn't say.

"How's Ms. Pat?" Soul asked after being quiet for so long. For a while there, he thought she'd been done talking for the night.

"My mother is still a badass," Micah said, unable to keep the grin from spreading across his mouth.

Soul giggled and relief flooded through him, effectively loosening some of the tension in the truck. She and his mother had gelled better than bread and butter, even to the point of his mother referring to Soul as her future daughter-in-law. Thankfully, she had never spoken those words to Soul, especially since they'd ended up going their separate ways.

To know his mother was to love her. Patricia Olsen had that type of personality that drew people to her with little effort. Funny, energetic, and the world's greatest cook, she loved throwing parties, traveling, and spending time with her friends.

"She's dating now," Micah said, giving a fake shiver which only made Soul laugh harder. "Nice guy, but it's just a little too weird watching them carry on like teenagers."

Micah's father, a former Atlanta police officer, had died years ago in the line of duty. As an only child, Micah had always been close to both of them but grew even closer to his mother after his father passed.

"Is he her age?" Soul asked.

"*Of course,* she wouldn't find someone her own age. This guy is in his mid- to late fifties. I think she said he was seven years younger than her."

"I'm not surprised. Last time I saw Ms. Pat, she looked at least ten years younger than she actually was. It's no wonder she caught the attention of a younger man."

They talked and laughed like old times, reminding Micah why he had fallen in love with her in the first place. He had always enjoyed hanging out with Soul. Even during their college days, whenever they were together, it had been easy to lose track of time and get lost in each other. Micah hadn't had that in a long time, and it was something he wanted again.

Too bad the timing of this reunion was all wrong. He had an assignment to see through. Yes, he needed to get close enough to Soul to make her want to spend more time with him. But he had no intention of losing his heart to her again. That was something he couldn't afford to do.

Micah finally turned onto her street and parked in front of the house. Atlanta was known for its horrific traffic, but tonight it hadn't been as bad. Yet, he had still managed to turn what should've been a fifteen-minute trip to her house into an hour, and he was glad he had. He enjoyed the conversation, and it was good to hear Soul laugh again.

"Listen, I'm sorry about tonight at the restaurant. I didn't mean to make you uncomfortable. There were some parts of the conversation I hadn't planned on sharing. It's just that…"

"It's just that you've always been good at expressing your feelings…your emotions."

Soul turned slightly in her seat toward him, her fresh scent wafting past his nose. When she rested her soft hand on his bare arm, Micah's body tightened. Need spread through him like a runaway locomotive, taking out everything in its path.

He was so screwed. Myles, for good reason, needed him to stay close to Soul. But their time together would be hard as hell if he didn't get a grip on his mind and body. It was just that everything about the woman—from her pretty face to her gentleness—did something to Micah. Drawn to Soul from the day they first met, it was as if nothing had changed. She had such a calm, loving spirit that could be felt in the way she looked at him, in the way she touched him, and even with her soothing words.

"I see you're still a straight shooter." Soul smiled at him, and his pulse amped up. "I loved that about you. I never had to wonder what you were thinking or how you felt about a situation."

Yeah, that trait was good and bad for him. He wasn't afraid to express his feelings, but that's partly why they had broken up. Micah had been honest with Soul, wanting her to know that he was crazy in love and wanted to spend the rest of his life with her. It hadn't been a proposal. Instead, his primary purpose of sharing what he'd felt for her while in college was to get a sense of where her head was at. Yes, he knew she had reservations about having children. He just hadn't realized that she hadn't wanted anything to do with marriage.

"I'm glad you told me how you feel," she continued. "I'm not gonna lie. You caught me off guard, but I can honestly say that you always have and always will have a special spot in my heart."

The last thing Micah intended to do was guilt her

into saying something she might not mean. It was definitely time to bring the night to an end.

"It's getting late," he said. "Sit tight, and I'll get the door for you."

Micah climbed out of the truck and released a long, cleansing breath as he glanced up at the dark sky, stars twinkling in the distance. Beautiful night. Gorgeous woman. Jacked-up situation. He had known it wouldn't be easy seeing Soul again. He just hadn't counted on it being this hard. Battling with past memories wasn't easy, but knowing that he was keeping something from her was also eating at him.

He opened the passenger door while Soul was still undoing her seat belt, and immediately his gaze went to her smooth bare legs and strappy sandals. Her white dress stopped just above her knees. But seated, the garment had inched up, teasing him with the sight of her dark, toned thighs. His body stirred, and all he wanted to do was start at her ankles and run his hand up her shapely legs. He'd work his way up her calf and wouldn't stop until he reached the apex between her firm thighs.

Damn. His thoughts were entering dangerous territory. No matter how he wanted it to be so, she wasn't his anymore. Soul would never be his again. Almost a year ago, she belonged to someone else. Someone she had planned to marry. Micah would do good to remember that.

When Soul started to climb out of the cab of the truck, he helped her down then closed the door. With his hand at the small of her back, Micah guided her up the walkway toward the house. For much of the night, he'd found every excuse to touch her. Having her this close to him as they walked side by side felt right. Felt perfect. A little too perfect.

Yep. I'm totally screwed.

When they arrived on the front porch, Soul pulled a set of keys out of her purse. Instead of looking at him, she glanced around at the quiet street. She and her roommates lived in the Grant Park area of Atlanta, a historic district that boasted stately homes and the fourth largest park in the city that held Zoo Atlanta.

"Micah, I…I um…" Soul started, her gaze now on the small ring of keys in her hand. When it seemed she couldn't get her words together, she shook her head as if having a private battle with herself. "Anyway, thank you for dinner." She started to walk away, but Micah stopped her with a hand on her arm.

As he pulled her close, Soul eyed him warily. Then her features softened. Micah wasn't sure what she saw on his face, but her shoulders also relaxed.

"Thanks for spending time with me," he said.

God, the woman smelled like heaven. His pulse pounded loudly in his ears as he longed to kiss her, especially with the way she stared into his eyes. Soul's soft hand cupped his cheek, and her gaze dropped to his mouth.

Ah, hell. He was defenseless when she looked at him like that. Like he hung the sun and the moon. All it would take was for him to lower his head and capture her mouth with his, but kissing Soul wasn't a good idea. Not when his emotions were a little too raw. And not when there were things she didn't know.

Micah stood frozen as she lifted up slightly and placed a lingering kiss on the corner of his mouth. So close to his lips that if he slanted his head the tiniest bit, their lips would touch. When she didn't pull away, a low rumble built inside of him and he gave up on the control that he'd barely been able to hang on to.

Before he could stop himself, Micah wrapped his arm around Soul's tiny waist and roughly pulled her against his body. She gasped in surprise but didn't push him away when he greedily captured her mouth. The searing lip-lock burned him to the core as he kissed her slowly, thoroughly, savoring every moment of her luscious mouth and boldly taking what he wanted.

His hand slid to the back of her neck, and his fingers tangled in her hair while he held her close. Having Soul in his arms again was like a dream come true, a fantasy that had played out in his mind more often than he could count. Passion swirled inside of him, and the intensity of the kiss sent blood rushing to a particular part of his anatomy while their tongues danced to a familiar beat.

This woman. This sweet and sexy woman had him feeling things he shouldn't be feeling. Especially when her body molded against his, filling him with a desire to have more, so much more of her. The kiss was everything Micah imagined it would be and then some.

Soft lips.

Sweetness.

A magnetic spark that could light up the darkest sky.

Right now, he wanted this woman more than he wanted his next breath, but damn. He shouldn't be kissing her. He shouldn't be loving how good and perfect Soul felt in his arms. He had an assignment to do, and it didn't include making out with this gorgeous woman.

Soul's small hands slowly slid up his torso and warmth radiated through Micah's shirt, lighting every nerve in his body on fire. A moan pierced the air, and he wasn't sure if it was from him or her. All he knew was that heat spread through his body like an out-of-control forest fire, and if he didn't put a stop to this soon, he wouldn't be able to.

He groaned roughly and slowly lifted his head and framed Soul's beautiful face within his hands. If only his conscience, his heart, and Myles's wrath weren't at stake. The goal was to stay alert and keep her close. Not suck on her lips and imagine what it would be like to be buried deep inside of her.

At the moment, he wanted to ignore that frantic voice inside of his head, warning him not to get too close. But it was too late. Soul Carrington would always be his even if he couldn't have her.

"I have missed you more than you would ever believe." Micah nibbled on her top lip, then her lower one. Clearly, he was a glutton for punishment because being this close to her was killing him. Yet, it was a struggle to let her go. "Get in the house before I do something I shouldn't do."

Like throw her over his shoulders and take her home with him, he thought.

After a slight hesitation, Soul pulled away, and Micah stood back and watched as she unlocked the door. She stepped across the threshold and glanced over her shoulder.

"Have a good night, Micah."

Yeah. That's not going to happen.

He was too wired. His body simmered with need, and he longed to have her in his life again in more ways than one.

After climbing into his truck, Micah knew what he had to do. He started the vehicle and made a call using the truck's Bluetooth. The phone rang several times through the speaker before the called was picked up.

"Yeah." The deep lazy drawl filled the interior of the truck.

"We need to talk," Micah said. "Tonight."

Chapter Five

*M*icah pulled into Supreme Security Agency's gated parking lot after being buzzed in and found a spot along the back row, as per Myles's instructions. The agency had people working around the clock, and Myles was on front desk duty. With potential clients showing up at all hours of the day, around-the-clock staff was needed.

Seconds after Micah parked, a light rap against the tinted passenger window snagged his attention. He unlocked the door.

"This better be good," Myles grumbled as he climbed into the cab of the truck, slamming the door. Dressed in a crisp black suit as well as a black dress shirt, he immediately started moving the knot of his black tie back and forth, loosening the neckwear. "What's so important that we had to meet tonight?"

"You're going to have to find someone else to look after Soul. I can't—"

"You can't what?" Myles asked gruffly. "You can't keep an eye on my sister, or you can't fall for her again?"

Since dropping Soul off at home almost an hour ago, Micah couldn't stop thinking about her. That earth-shattering kiss didn't help matters. He could still taste her sweetness. Still recall the softness of her body molded against his. There was no way he could do what Myles was asking and not fall for her all over again. It was fine to love Soul from a distance, but...

His willpower when it came to the woman was nonexistent. Micah wanted her back in every way a man could want a woman, and that bothered him. Soul could hurt him in ways his time in the military never could, and she probably had no clue to the power she wielded.

Micah leaned back against the headrest and huffed out a breath, feeling like a punk for not being able to keep his emotions in check. It had always been that way when it came to Soul, and tonight was no different. He had made a fool of himself at dinner. Thankfully, she hadn't held his anger from earlier against him if the way she returned his kiss was any indication.

He shook his head. He couldn't risk getting his heart crushed. Kissing Soul again was like going back in time. The passionate feelings that swirled inside of him, consuming his whole being, was like nothing he'd ever experienced. Not even when they dated. Not even with his wife. The need for more from Soul was too strong to ignore. If he wanted to maintain his sanity and protect his heart, there was no way he'd be able to spend time with her as planned.

"Well?" Myles prompted, irritation in his tone as he pulled Micah back into the conversation. "What's the problem? I would think you'd be glad to spend some time with her."

"Not if I have to lie to her." Not telling her the real reason he suddenly showed up at the dance studio felt wrong on so many levels. He couldn't betray her by keeping information from her that she really should know.

"I didn't ask you to lie. I asked you to be my backup when I'm on a job and can't get to my sister. All you have to do is look out for her until I figure out what's going on with Ryan. Few months, tops."

"And where are you on that?"

"I have someone watching him. Right now, Ryan is in Dallas. He's been moving around for the last nine months, and we're still trying to determine if he's in contact with Ebolsa. If he is, this might be the only way to finally get the elusive weapons dealer behind bars where he belongs. We stay close to Ryan; he'll lead us to Ebolsa."

"Who is we?"

Myles hesitated in responding, which spoke volumes. Even if he wasn't officially employed with the CIA any longer, Micah had a feeling he still either did work for them or kept in touch with someone. He always had his finger on the pulse of all things corrupt, which was probably how he found out that Soul's ex-fiancé, Ryan, was doing business with a known gun smuggler.

"Are you still with the CIA?" Micah asked.

"No," Myles said, looking Micah dead in the eyes. There was no telling if he was being truthful. The guy had been a spy for so long, lying was second nature. Not even a lie detector could trip him up. "But there's nothing I wouldn't do to protect my family, even force Ryan, the bastard, to walk away from my sister without telling her why."

Micah gave a slow nod as he continued studying Myles. Soul admitted to not loving Ryan enough. Clearly, the feelings had been mutual. Because if it were Micah in the man's shoes, nothing or no one would've been able to pull him away from Soul.

He broke eye contact with Myles and stared out the front window as he replayed that last thought in his mind. Who was he to judge the man? Like Ryan, Micah had given up too quickly on keeping Soul in his life.

You should've fought for me, Soul's words filtered into his mind. Had he fought harder to keep them together, would it have mattered? Would she have eventually changed her mind about marriage and children? He would never know. Unfortunately, back then, all he could think about was protecting himself. Even now, Soul might claim to be ready to settle down, but Micah wasn't sure he was buying it. It could be that she didn't love Ryan enough because deep down she really didn't want marriage and a family.

"I think Soul agreed to marry Ryan because she was lonely," Myles said as if reading Micah's mind. "The guy was a good actor. Seeing her as an easy mark, he played to her weaknesses. She's still a softy, willing to take in any stray whether it has four legs or two, and he was definitely a stray."

Still staring out the front window, Micah recalled a number of instances where Soul had done just that. Like when they were picnicking in the park, and she'd found a kitten. Insisting on keeping the animal, she had taken it home, but her roommates nixed the idea. Soul had been prepared to move out if they insisted on her getting rid of the cat. Thankfully, it worked out, and she found a family who adopted it.

She was loveable, kind, and had one of the gentlest spirits of anyone he knew. On more than one occasion, he'd seen people try to take advantage of her. How she came out so sweet and innocent but had a brother like Myles had always been a mystery to Micah.

"How did she meet Ryan?"

Micah could feel Myles's gaze on him but kept his attention on the darkness outside the window.

"What did she tell you?"

Now Micah was the one who was slow to respond. Usually a private person, he rarely shared his own information. There was no way he planned on telling Myles any of the conversation he'd had with Soul.

"Not much. Why don't you fill me in on what I don't know?"

"Why? If you can't do me this solid, why should I tell your punk ass anything? You're ready to walk away, possibly leave her vulnerable because you're scared. Of what, I don't know, but I'm starting to think I should've recruited someone else. As a matter of fact, I can think of a couple of guys who'd love to spend some time with her."

Micah leveled him with a glare, anger slowly rising to the surface. He didn't like games, and sometimes dealing with Myles seemed like one big mind game. "You know how I feel about her. Otherwise, you wouldn't have come to me with any of this. So quit screwing around and just tell me. How did they meet?"

"She hit him with her car."

Micah frowned and turned in his seat to directly look at Myles. "What?"

"You heard me." Myles's lips twitched, fighting off a smile. "Soul ran into him with her car. You know she can't drive worth shit, and Ryan found out the hard way. It was a good thing she was driving slowly. Otherwise, the accident could've been worse than him ending up with a broken leg and a sprained wrist."

Micah narrowed his gaze at the man he considered a friend...well, maybe an associate. "Are you serious?"

"As a heart attack." Myles chuckled, shaking his head as he loosened his tie a little more.

"How the hell does someone go from running someone down with their car to getting engaged to him?"

"Only my sister can run over a guy and then make him fall in love with her."

Micah sat stunned and listened as Myles relayed all he knew about the incident, including how Soul had stayed at the hospital long after Ryan got out of surgery. Which sounded like something she would do. Soul had always cared more for others than she had herself. Even if she hadn't been the one to hit Ryan, but had seen the accident, she was the type to make sure everyone involved was okay.

"Long story short, Ryan didn't have any family, and Soul took it upon herself to nurse him back to health. Three months later, she called to tell me she planned to marry the asshole. I didn't like him the moment I met him."

Micah snorted. "That's not saying much. There are not too many people you like, especially when it comes to those who date your sister."

When she and Micah dated, Myles hadn't given him too much of a hard time. Except he did threaten to kick his ass if he ever hurt Soul. He had also vowed to cut off Micah's man parts if he got Soul pregnant.

Micah smirked at the memory. Back then, he believed her brother would do just that. Hell, he probably still would.

"Listen, man. I get that you feel some kind of way

about Soul, and I'm cool with that. I'm not asking you to betray her. I'm just asking that you keep her close. Ham's putting me on a covert assignment that's going to have me tied up awhile," Myles said of his boss, Hamilton Crosby, the manager of Supreme Security-Atlanta. "I need someone looking out for Soul in case she gets caught in the crosshairs of whatever Ryan is wrapped up in."

"Why not just tell her what's going on, or what you think is going on? Why all of the secrecy? Soul deserves to know if her life *might* be in danger."

"No need to upset her if we don't have to. My sister has a soft spot for Ryan. The guy could tell her anything, and she'd believe him."

Micah shook his head. "You're not giving her enough credit. If you told her what you know about Ryan, I'm sure she'll believe you over anything he says."

"Maybe, but maybe not. When she told me she was marrying the loser, I did a background check on the guy. He had given her too many half-truths, and no matter what I told her, he always had an answer to explain my concerns away. For instance, Ryan told her he was an accountant for a software company in Houston. Turned out, he hadn't worked for them in two years. When she questioned him about it, he told her that he was too embarrassed to admit that he'd been laid off from the company. At least she had sense enough to question him about how he was making a living. How he was able to afford a luxury apartment in one of Houston's most expensive neighborhoods."

"What did he say?"

"He told her that he was a virtual accounting assistant for several small business owners, and business was going well. He was even able to afford a small office space and managed their books. Of course, I dug a little deeper, but the guy is good. It took me months to trace him to Ebolsa and determine that he wasn't only managing the man's books, but also laundering money for him."

"And instead of reporting Ryan, you made him break things off with Soul so that you and whoever you're working with could get him to lead you to his boss."

"Yeah, something like that," Myles admitted, no remorse in his tone.

It bugged the hell out of Micah how the Feds and even the CIA sometimes risked innocent people's well-being in order to make a big catch. Didn't sound as if Ryan was an innocent in any of this, but he was a small fish in an ocean full of sharks.

"To be honest, I think the guy was really in love with Soul, but he's a spineless bastard. I put a little fear in him. Told him that if he didn't quietly break things off with her, not only would the Feds receive an anonymous tip, but that Ebolsa would know that Ryan was a leak in his organization."

"And you think because of his feelings for Soul, Ryan will eventually try to get in contact with her even though it's been a year."

Myles nodded. "Or I think he'll do something stupid

and Ebolsa will hunt down anyone attached to Ryan. Even if he and Soul are no longer together, I can't take the risk that they won't somehow pull Soul into this mess. Hell, for all I know, he might still be in touch with her."

"He's not," Micah volunteered. "She hasn't heard from him."

"You sure about that?"

"That's what she told me. She said he disappeared and she hasn't heard from him since."

"Yeah, let's just hope it stays that way. So you in or out?"

Micah released a slow, frustrated breath. He would never forgive himself if anything happened to Soul, and the worst thing that could happen to him was that he lost his heart to the woman again. But…

"Well?" Myles prompted.

"I'm in."

Chapter Six

"Okay, ladies, let's do a few foot exercises. Have a seat on the floor. Melissa, would you mind demonstrating?" Soul asked the other instructor.

The dance studio had been opened a few days now, and Soul couldn't be more pleased. Already she had six full classes and a couple of others that were slowly getting there. One of the best decisions she had made regarding the business venture was taking over an existing business. Having a built-in clientele was priceless. Melissa, who initially worked for the previous owners, had made the deal even sweeter by agreeing to stay on and work for Soul.

While Melissa took her position at the front of the class, so that all ten girls could easily see her, Soul moved around the room where they were sitting on the floor. In Houston, she typically taught older children, but she loved working with her younger groups. The three-year-olds through five-year-olds were all so adorable, and she could already spot her future superstars.

"Backs straight. No slouching. You have to sit up nice and tall." She roamed around the group, checking on everyone's posture. "Now let's start with our right foot. Flex…point. Flex…point."

For the next few minutes, Soul assisted those who needed a little extra help while Melissa gave additional instructions. After a while, Soul left the group to get caught up on paperwork. First, she needed to follow up with a plumber who was supposed to have been there earlier and still hadn't arrived.

She headed down the hallway that led to her office but stopped when the front door opened. A smile spread across her face as Micah walked in, carrying a white bag.

"Hey, you," she said when he got closer, and they were out of earshot of the class. Soul didn't think she would ever get tired of seeing him. Every day since the night they'd had dinner and shared that toe-curling kiss, Micah had either called or stopped by. He was quickly becoming the highlight of her days.

"This is a pleasant surprise."

"I figured you might be hungry." He held up the bag. "Do you have time for a quick lunch?"

He wrapped his long arm around her and placed a kiss against her temple. It was sweet, but Soul would rather feel his lips on her mouth. For whatever reason, he was set on keeping their interactions PG, and that would be okay if she weren't interested in more.

"I do, and this is perfect timing. I just need to call the plumber." Micah walked alongside her as they headed to her office. "The guy was supposed to be here first thing this morning and still hasn't shown up."

"What's going on with the plumbing?" Micah stepped aside and let her enter the office first, and Soul closed the door once they were inside.

"The water pressure is too low, and I'm not sure how to fix it. I thought maybe the city was doing work in the neighborhood, but neither of my neighbors are having a problem."

Soul sat in the leather chair behind her desk. While making her phone call, she watched as Micah pulled items out of the bag. He set a small salad and apple juice near her, and a hamburger and fries were placed on the other side of the desk where he was sitting.

He had always been attentive, knowing what she liked and didn't like. Or what she ate and rarely ate, and that attentiveness hadn't wavered. He was still the most thoughtful man she'd ever met.

Just when she thought the plumber was going to answer, his voicemail greeting started.

Hi, this is Roy. Unfortunately, I'm either on the other line or on a job. Leave your name and number, and I'll return your call. Have a nice day.

Soul didn't bother leaving a message. She had already left three. The saying *good help is hard to find* definitely referred to him. The first time he had come out was to install a new toilet in the bathroom, and he had done an excellent job. She figured she'd use his services again.

"No answer, huh?"

Soul shook her head. "Voicemail. I'll give him until the end of the day. After that, I'll have to find someone else. Or better yet, maybe you can pay him a visit wearing your uniform and put the fear of God in him."

Soul had only seen him in his police uniform once and had almost lost her mind. The man was irresistibly gorgeous in regular clothes but in uniform...*Lord*. He'd been breathtakingly sexy with a fierceness that brought all of her women parts to life.

Micah chuckled. "I'll add him to my patrol schedule tonight." He winked and glanced at his watch. "Speaking of schedule, I'm going to have to make this visit a little short. My shift starts in an hour."

Soul stared at Micah's French fries and her mouth watered. Typically, her meals consisted of grains, fruits, and vegetables, but every once in a while, she craved fries. The crunchy exterior with the delicate interior and just the right amount of salt on them did her in every time. They were her guilty pleasure. And Micah knew it. Which was probably why he was torturing her and eating them slowly, making sure to wave one around before stuffing it into his mouth.

She narrowed her eyes at him. "How can you be so cruel?"

He burst out laughing. "Wh-what? I have no idea what you're talking about."

"I can't believe you're going to sit there and lie, and then you don't even offer me one."

"Aw, poor baby. I'm trying to save you from yourself. I know one will never be enough for you. But here, I'll let you have a little taste." He reached across the desk and slowly fed her a long, crispy one and Soul tried not to moan, but couldn't contain herself as she chewed.

"You're right. One will never be enough."

Smiling, he shook his head and dug into the bag. "Then it's a good thing I ordered you some."

"Micah…" Soul's hand went to her heart, and she stopped short of telling him that she loved him. "You're too good to me."

"Yeah, right. A minute ago, you were calling me a liar, but I won't hold it against you. It's gotta be hard living on just lettuce."

She grinned, stuffing two fries into her mouth and relishing every single salted, grease-laden nibble. It had been months since she treated herself, and Soul planned to enjoy every single morsel.

"How do you like being a police officer?" she asked, halfway through her fries. She hated the fact that he was a cop, but would never tell him that.

"It's all right. Like every job, it has its good and bad, and ups and downs, but I like knowing that I'm making a difference."

"What's your least favorite part? What type of calls make you cringe when you get them?"

"All of them, but mainly domestic violence calls." He

shook his head. "I think almost every cop will list those types of calls as one of their top three least favorites to get."

Listening to him explain how they never knew what they were walking in on caused Soul's heart rate to spike. The thought of people who claim to have once loved each other going at it to the point of having to call the police was mind-boggling.

"Sometimes we'll show up, and all that's happening is a heated argument. Other times someone might be swinging a skillet around—or even worse, a knife. Those type of situations tend to escalate before either party realizes just how bad it's gotten. Then, unfortunately, we usually have to haul one of them away in cuffs."

"God, that has to be awful, especially if kids are there." Soul didn't have the stomach for all that law enforcement had to deal with. Just hearing about some of the incidents made her skin crawl. "What's your favorite part of the job?"

"Helping old ladies across the street."

Soul's fork stopped inches from her mouth, and she stared at him. He said it without missing a beat, and she wasn't sure if he was serious or kidding. At least not until he smiled.

"You'd be amazed at the good deeds we end up doing, even helping folks across the street."

For the next few minutes, they talked and laughed as they ate, hopping from one topic to the next. She had known that his father used to be a cop but hadn't known that was the case for his grandfather, too.

"Have you ever considered doing something different? Something like what Myles does for Supreme Security? You could be one of *Atlanta's Finest*," Soul said between bites of salad. "Then again, I guess you already are."

Micah flashed that sexy grin that sent goosebumps raking over her flesh. Man, she had it bad for this guy.

"Actually, Myles mentioned that Supreme was recruiting, and practically guaranteed that I'd get hired. So, doing personal security is definitely an option."

Soul knew that the city needed police officers, but knowing Micah was risking his life everyday bothered her. There was so much craziness in the world, it would kill her if anything ever happened to him. She loved the idea of them rekindling their relationship, but didn't know if she could date a cop.

Micah finished off his burger and started stuffing the empty wrappers into the bag the items had come in.

"You know, if you keep surprising me with these wonderful lunches, you're going to spoil me."

"I like the idea of spoiling you," he said just before gulping down some of his lemonade.

Every time he made those sweet sentiments, her heart flipped in response. Yet, there were moments when she felt as if he was holding himself back. Soul loved that he called or stopped by. She just wished that she had a better read on where this…this, whatever was building between them, was going.

Patience, the small voice inside her head cautioned as she drank her apple juice. It took time to rebuild the type of relationship they once had, but her heart and body were impatient. The man stirred something so uncontrollably promiscuous within her. Each time they were together, Soul wanted to strip down and throw herself at him.

"Why are you looking at me like that?" he asked, and Soul choked on her apple juice.

Coughing, she set the bottle down and patted her chest as if that would clear her airway. Micah started to stand, concern marring his face, but Soul shook her head and waved him back into his seat.

"I'm okay," she croaked, still coughing. "The juice just went down wrong."

"You sure you're okay?"

She nodded and wiped the tears from her eyes. "I'm fine."

"So those must have been some X-rated thoughts rolling around in that pretty little head of yours. My simple question got you all choked up."

"They were." She laughed, and one of his brows shot up. "I'm thinkin' I should probably just keep those thoughts to myself until we're somewhere a little more private."

"I see. Now I'm intrigued." He glanced at his watch

again. "Unfortunately, I don't have time to dig deeper since I need to get going."

He stood, and Soul's heart dropped. She hated that their time together was so short.

"Are you working every night this week?"

Micah tossed their trash into the container next to the desk. "Yeah, we've been on mandatory overtime for the past couple of weeks. Hopefully, things will die down soon."

"I hope so." Soul walked around the desk and stopped in front of him. "I would love it if you and I could have dinner again or maybe take in a movie."

"That can definitely be arranged." Micah slid his arm around her waist and pulled her against his hard body, sending a sweet thrill rushing through her. "By the way, I'm loving the outfit. You have that whole ballerina thing going on," he said of the pink leotard with a matching tutu that she wore whenever teaching her younger children. "It's kinda hot."

Soul's eyes drifted closed, and she moaned with pleasure at the heady sensation his lips were causing as he planted feathery kisses along her neck. "Good to know," she said breathily. "I'll have to wear a similar one when it's just you and me. One that I think you'll really appreciate."

He slowly lifted his head and looked at her. "Can't wait."

Again, he was holding back. If the way he was eyeing her mouth was any indication, it was clear he wanted to kiss her. Yet, all he did was stand there, his hands framing her face while looking indecisive.

Soul slid her hands over his hard abs and up his chest, enjoying the way his muscles rippled beneath her touch. Raising up on tiptoes, she wrapped her arms around his neck and covered his mouth with hers. Sometimes you just had to take what you wanted.

She might've started the kiss, but Micah quickly took over. His kiss was urgent, yet exploratory as his tongue tangled with hers, Soul gave herself freely, loving the way he hungrily ravished her mouth. He had always been able to spark something so reckless within her, making her want more than just his kisses. This time was no different. It was only a matter of time before they took this attraction to the next level.

Micah moaned against her mouth and mumbled something that she couldn't decipher before slowly ending the kiss.

"Damn, woman. You do something to me," he said in a husky tone and touched his forehead to hers. Breathing hard, their breaths mingled as they each attempted to get air into their lungs. "I could stay here kissing you forever, but I'd better go before I'm late."

After a quick peck on the lips, he backed away. Soul loved their times together, but it was getting harder to say goodbye to him. Which was crazy. They'd been apart for years. Yet now, even being away from him for a few hours was like torture.

"Call me later, no matter the time," she said as he left the office.

"Will do."

Micah dug his keys from his pocket and slipped on his sunglasses the moment he stepped out of the building. He had known he was playing with fire when he pulled Soul into his arms. But he couldn't help himself. Her scent, her laughter, even her cute little ballerina outfit had turned him on. *And that kiss.* He'd been powerless when she touched her lips to his.

Micah blew out a frustrated breath, and he glanced around the parking lot on the way to his truck. He needed a better plan as far as Soul was concerned. It wasn't a hardship spending time with her. Heck, he actually looked forward to it. But it killed him each time he had to leave.

More now than ever, Micah wanted to come clean about Ryan. Only he had no idea how Soul would respond. It could go a number of different ways. She could be glad he told her and then welcome the opportunity to have him and her brother watching her back. Or she would be pissed that he and Myles—mainly Myles—had butted into her life. Then there was a chance that she might not talk to either of them for keeping this information from her. And then there was one more scenario that Micah didn't want to entertain. She could find out from someone else and think he'd been playing her since the moment he showed up at her studio.

That option bothered him the most. He already knew that he wanted her back in his life, but she might see it as him just trying to do a solid for Myles. See it as him playing with her and her feelings.

"I'm screwed no matter how I look at it," Micah mumbled as he climbed into his truck.

Whatever he decided to do, it needed to be soon because their kisses were getting hotter, and his need for her more intense.

My little ballerina. My sexy-as-sin ballerina.

He couldn't lose her again, and he'd be damned if he let dealing with Myles or Ryan mess up this second chance with her.

She's mine.

Chapter Seven

*S*oul hurried into the bar and grill where she was meeting her roommates for dinner and drinks. She hoped that one of them had arrived early enough to snag a booth. Being thirty minutes late, thanks to one of the pipes bursting at the studio, had her irritation level at an all-time high. The last thing she needed was another expense, but what she wanted was a stiff drink to help her relax.

She moved further into the dimly-lit space as one of Beyoncé's latest hits pumped through the speakers. Even in three-inch heels, she couldn't see over the multitude of people spread throughout. Easing around a group standing at a belly bar table, Soul searched the crowd for Janice's wild auburn curls. That's who she usually spotted first.

"Hey, beautiful. You lookin' for me?" a handsome man with gorgeous hazel eyes asked.

"No. Sorry." She moved around him. Too bad he didn't look a day over sixteen. Otherwise, she might've engaged in conversation. Then again, probably not. There was only one man she wouldn't mind talking to, and she was trying to put him out of her head, at least for the night.

"You sure? I'd love to get to know you better," the same guy said, his hand loosely gripping her elbow.

Soul pulled out of his grasp. "Positive. Now excuse me."

She didn't give him a chance to say anything else. Instead of continuing to the back of the building where more tables and booths were located, she made a beeline for the bar. She wasn't much of a drinker, but between having a busted pipe, water damage, and constant thoughts of Micah and his sexy lips, her nerves were stretched thin.

They'd spent time together over the last couple of weeks, only making Soul fall for him all over again. The more time she spent with the man, the more time she wanted to spend with him. But she couldn't get a good read on Micah. One minute he made her feel as if he'd love for them to be a couple again. Then the next, he was putting up a wall. Soul couldn't figure him out.

"I need a drink for real," she mumbled to herself. Every spot at the bar was occupied, but she was able to squeeze between two guys to reach the bar. "Sorry," she said to a stocky man fully covering one of the stools.

"No apology necessary. Let me buy you a drink, and

you can have my seat," he said close to her ear. She barely heard him over the loud music pumping through a large nearby speaker.

"That won't be necessary, but thanks."

She waved her arm to get the bartender's attention. Despite mixing a drink, he gave her a head-nod, letting her know that he saw her. Minutes later, he set a napkin down in front of her.

"What can I get you, sweetheart?"

Usually, she'd order a glass of wine, but tonight she needed something stronger. "A Long Island iced tea."

"Coming right up."

The moment he walked away to prepare the drink, Soul pulled her cell phone from her bag and noticed a text message from Janice.

We're at a booth in the back.

Oh, good. They were already there.

With her drink in hand, Soul skirted around pockets of people and headed to the back of the building. She spotted her roommates immediately.

"Hey, you guys. Sorry I'm late." She gave Janice a quick hug but scooted in next to Jada since Janice had her motorcycle helmet sitting in the seat next to her. "I thought you said you weren't going to ride late at night."

"Tonight's an exception. I didn't get a chance to go home and get my car."

Soul referred to Janice as her adventurous friend, willing to try any and everything at least once. She'd been riding motorcycles for as long as Soul could remember. No matter how much she and Jada worried about her, Janice was going to do her own thing.

"Well, if it isn't my favorite ladies brightening up the place," their server Anthony said. They seemed to always end up at one of his tables, and Soul had no complaints. He often bought them a drink or gave them a complimentary appetizer whenever they showed up.

"Well, if it isn't one of my favorite men," Janice flirted, giving him a wink before they all placed their order.

Soul shook her head. The man was in lust with Janice, and she knew it. Always flirting with him, though she had no intention of giving him any play. Especially now that she had reconnected with Nathan, a nice guy she had dated years ago before moving to California.

A short while later, Anthony returned with a glass of wine for Jada, club soda for Janice, and another Long Island iced tea for Soul. He also set a basket of teriyaki chicken wings and chips and salsa in the center of the table.

"And these are on me," he said, adding a plate of potato skins to the already crowded tabletop.

"You're a sweetheart," Janice said.

Soul had been looking forward to tonight all day. Every month the three of them met up for a girl's night. Sometimes they went out on the town, while other times they'd hang out at home. The month before, Jada, who wasn't much of a cook, whipped up one of Solomon's award-winning recipes. It was no wonder he was the latest winning master chef on one of the Food Channel's most popular shows. His meals were amazing.

"Let's make a toast," Janice said, and they each lifted their glasses. "Here's to fun times, dreams coming true—"

"And finding a love of a lifetime," Jada added, and Soul's mind immediately went to thoughts of Micah as they all clinked glasses.

A love of a lifetime.

Was it too crazy to hope that they could find their way back to each other? Since the night he had confessed that he never stopped loving her, one thing was for sure. The passion they shared years ago was stronger than ever now. More than anything, Soul wanted a second chance with Micah. She wanted him to fill that void that he had created when he walked out of her life all those years ago.

"So, did you see Micah today?" Janice asked in a singsong voice as if she were a mind-reader.

Soul finished off her first drink and started on the second one. "No, but I talked to him earlier. I just don't know what to make of the guy. That very first night we went out, I thought he was mad at me for agreeing to marry Ryan, but when I—"

"I still can't wrap my brain around him being mad at that. He's the one who walked away in college. He's lucky you're even giving him the time of day," Jada said, loading her small plate up with wings.

"Says the woman who won't admit that she's madly

in love with her *friend*." Janice used air quotes when she said friend.

Jada pointed a celery stick at her. "Don't start unless you want me to go there with you about Nathan." That shut Janice up, and Soul smiled.

All three of them longed for that once-in-a-lifetime kind of love. An unparalleled love that exceeded all understanding. But it seemed each was afraid to hope or admit that the men currently in their lives could be that person to give them what they desired most.

For Soul, Micah was saying all the right things about wanting to spend time with her so they could get to know each other again. Yet, he had his guard up where she was concerned, and that's what she explained to her friends. However, she still hadn't come clean to them about why she and Micah broke up in the first place.

"Until you're positive about what you want from him, Micah is going to continue keeping you at arm's length," Jada said. "He's probably picking up on your indecisive vibe. You want him back, but I think you don't trust your judgment after what happened with Ryan. Besides, I'm not sure you really loved your ex."

Soul frowned. "What?" She hadn't mentioned to either of them her revelation regarding Ryan.

"You might've thought you loved him, but not like Micah," Jada continued. "It took you forever to get over losing him. As for Ryan, he was someone who caught you at a vulnerable time."

Soul's mouth dropped open, and her gaze bounced between her two friends.

"Don't look so surprised," Janice said. "We knew. Even when you called us to discuss the wedding plans, you didn't talk about him the way you used to go on and on about Micah."

"And you were going to let me marry the guy?" Soul asked, shocked at what she was hearing.

Jada looked at her sideways. "Did I not ask you a thousand times if you were sure about marrying him?"

"Yeah, but…" Soul couldn't say anything. They were right on all accounts. At the time, she thought she was in love with Ryan. "I thought you guys liked him."

Janice made a face, twisting her mouth as if she smelled something bad. "He was all right, but you're different with Micah. Besides, you didn't look at Ryan the way you drool over Micah."

Soul laughed and kicked her under the table. "I do not drool over him."

"Actually," Jada started before wiping her mouth with a napkin, "when he stopped by last night, and the night he took you to dinner, girl, you were drooling."

"I'm not listening to this. Let's talk about something else."

As her friends chatted, Soul thought about what they'd said. When she was around Micah, her heart beat double-time, and she was always in a state of arousal. Not just because he was gorgeous. It was everything about him. The power he exuded. The way he looked at her. More importantly, it was the way she felt when she was in his presence. Being with him felt…right.

But if Soul was honest, she was scared of getting closer. Scared that if she and Micah managed to truly find their way back to each other, she might not still be able to give him what he wanted—marriage and a family. She wasn't afraid to get married, but she'd be lying if she didn't admit that every now and then the thought of having a baby freaked her out. What if she ended up like her mother and died during childbirth?

That thought made her consider something else. Maybe she had fallen for Ryan so fast because he hadn't wanted children. It was just going to be the two of them, building a life together.

Well, that's never going to happen. It was amazing how the best-laid plans could change at any given moment. Soul just hoped the next stages of her life would continue to bring her all that she desired.

For the next hour, she faded in and out of the conversation with her girls. She was definitely more relaxed than she'd been when first arriving. Good discussions and good food and drinks went a long way in turning a bad day into a great night.

"I'm gonna have to bail out on you guys a little early tonight. I promised to help Solomon with something," Jada said, digging into her handbag and pulling out her wallet.

"Put that away," Janice told her. "I'm treating tonight."

"I should've known you'd be seeing your *best friend*. You're even more dolled up than usual," Soul said, looking her up and down. Her friend always dressed to impress, but tonight she looked even cuter. "Exactly what type of help do you have to give big, strong, sexy Solomon?"

Jada and Solomon had been friends for a long time, and Soul couldn't understand why they just wouldn't claim each other as more than friends. It was clear to anyone who saw them together that they were in love.

"Fine. If you must know. I'm attending a party that the mayor is having. Solomon catered dinner for her a couple of days ago, and she invited him and a guest to stop through tonight." Jada shrugged. "I'm his guest."

"Ooh la la. And just think, I thought you dressed up for us," Janice cracked.

They all laughed and as usual, started talking at once. Soul ordered another drink, and for another thirty minutes, conversation flowed smoothly. They all were so busy lately that there were some days they didn't see each other, even though they lived in the same house.

Anthony strolled over to the table with an empty round tray under his arm. "Can I get you beautiful women anything else?"

"I'll have another." Soul lifted her almost-empty glass, and Anthony nodded before slipping away.

"Wait. That'll be your fourth Long Island iced tea. Don't you think you've had enough?" Jada asked. She was the momma bear of the trio and never let them forget.

"I know, *mommy*," Soul said in a tiny mocking voice, her words a little slurred.

It was a Saturday night, and she was going to have to be in that big house all by herself since both Janice and Jada had additional plans for the night. Why not have another drink?

"The drink Ant—Anthony brings back will be my last. Pro—promise. And fu—fuss at Jan. She had a lot to drink, too."

"Oh, God. You're drunk, and for your information, this is club soda." Janice shook her head. "Your little ol' self never could hold your liquor."

Soul sat up straighter but squinted at her friend when the room started spinning a little. She blinked several times until her friend came into better view. "I'm not drunk...tipsy maybe, but not drunk." Her goal had been to block out all the drama from the day and try to get Micah out of her mind. The liquor was definitely helping, mostly.

"Where are your car keys?" Jada dug around in Soul's handbag until she found them. "You're not driving. I'll get Solomon to drop you off at home before we go to his event."

"Or I can strap her to the back of my bike." Janice grinned. "That'll sober her up."

"I'm n—not drunk, and there's no—no way I'm

getting on th—that death trap." Soul turned to Jada but gripped the table when she started seeing double.

Okay, maybe I'll drink a little slower.

"I did—didn't drive," she said. "I Ubered."

Soul got halfway through the drink that Anthony sat in front of her when she started feeling the effects of it. She closed her eyes and gripped her head with both hands. Maybe the girls were right. Maybe this last one was one too many.

"I fe—felt fine 'til you heffas said something about me being drunk. Now the ring—ringing in my head won't st —stop."

Her friends burst out laughing.

"Girl, that's my phone." Jada held up the device before answering it.

Soul could barely focus but heard bits and pieces of the conversation. It sounded like Solomon was outside.

"All right, Soul. He's here. Get up so we can get going." Jada nudged her, only making Soul's head spin more.

"You go ahead. We're going to hang out a little longer. I'll make sure our girl gets home safely," Janice said. An hour later, she waved Anthony over for the check. "Soul, unlock your phone and give it to me."

"Why?"

"Because I'm gonna call you a ride."

Chapter Eight

*J*arred awake by the ringing of his cell phone, Micah didn't bother opening his eyes. He reached his arm out and patted around on top of the nightstand until his hand landed on the device.

"Hello," he answered, barely able to get past the sleep fog that was slowly pulling him back under. He'd had to work another double and had crashed the moment he got home a few hours ago.

"Come get your girl," the person on the other end of the line said. "She needs a ride home."

Micah cracked his eyes open and squinted at the clock on the nightstand. *One a.m.* Then he pulled the cell phone away from his ear and glanced at the screen.

Soul.

He bolted upright. "What the... Who is this?"

"This is Jan, and I'm sure—"

Jan? Then it dawned on him; her roommate. "Where is Soul?" he asked more gruffly than intended, unable to keep the panic out of his voice. He sat on the edge of the bed as various scenarios ran through his mind, none of them good.

"What's going on? Is she all right?"

"It depends on your definition of all right. Physically, your girl is fine, but she's had a little too much to drink and can barely stand. I did manage to keep her from face-planting a minute ago, but you should come and get her."

Now wide awake, Micah quickly slipped into the pair of jeans that lay on the floor nearby and grabbed a clean T-shirt from the laundry basket. He didn't bother asking Janice why she couldn't get Soul home. Instead, he asked for the address before hanging up.

Fifteen minutes later, Micah pulled up to the popular Midtown bar. He spotted Janice first, a motorcycle helmet in one hand and a purse dangling in the other. Soul was sitting on one of the concrete steps that led to the bar's entrance. She was slumped over, her head resting on her knees.

How had "I'm hanging with the girls tonight" ended up with her getting drunk? She didn't drink. Maybe a glass of wine here and there, but never anything stronger. At least as far as Micah knew. Clearly, there were things he didn't know.

He parked in front of the building and hopped out of his truck.

"Thanks for coming," Janice said when he approached them. "I would've gotten her home, but I'm on my bike." She nodded toward the Harley parked a few feet away.

"So, you still ride, huh?"

She grinned. "Every chance I get."

"I'm assuming that if you're using that mode of transportation that you haven't been drinking."

"No, sir, officer. Not a lick of alcohol tonight." She smirked.

Micah chuckled. "Good to know." He turned his attention to Soul who hadn't moved or made a sound. "Exactly how many drinks did she have tonight?"

"Four Long Island iced teas."

Micah whistled. He rarely had more than one of those at a time, and with Soul's body weight, her alcohol level was probably through the roof.

He sat on the step next to her and wrapped his arm around her to shield her from a few people plowing out of the bar. Their raucous laughter and the way they staggered out of the building had him wondering if they were trashed, too.

"Why'd you guys let her drink so much?" he asked Janice while gently rubbing Soul's back.

"She's a grown woman who does what she wants. Besides, she had some things to work out."

Micah glanced up. "Things? Things like what?"

"For starters, you."

He pointed at himself. "Me?"

"Yeah, you. That's why I called you. Figured you could use this opportunity to spend more time together. Ask a few questions. Determine what's rolling around in that head of hers. You might be surprised at what you find out. Although, you might want to sober her up first."

All Micah could do was stare at Soul's friend. What problems could Soul be trying to drown out? And what could they possibly have to do with him? Had she heard from Ryan? Did she know what he was involved in?

Micah shook those last thoughts free. Knowing what her ex was involved in wouldn't start her to drinking. She'd be trying to hunt him down for answers.

"Soul?" He gently shook her, assuming she had dozed off since she still hadn't moved.

Her head shot up, barely missing Micah's chin. "I'm not drunk." Then she groaned and gripped the sides of her head. "God, make it stop," she whined.

"How about I take you home?"

Her gaze shot to Micah, a bewildered expression marring her beautiful face. Seconds ticked by before she spoke.

"Hi."

"Hi yourself. So, you're not drunk, huh?" he asked, unable to keep the humor from his tone. Damn, she was cute, even if she struggled to keep her head steady. "All right, Ms. Prissy. Let's get you out of here."

Micah helped her stand, but when she wobbled, he scooped her up into his arms. She felt lighter than she'd been in college.

"I can walk," she said weakly and laid her head against his chest before closing her eyes. "I can walk."

"I know, baby, but I prefer carrying you."

"That's why I love you. I'll always love you," she whispered, but Micah heard her loud and clear. Part of him was thrilled to hear the words. The other part of him hoped she remembered them in the morning. Then again, maybe it would be better if she didn't.

Before he could get her settled into the front seat of his truck, Soul was sound asleep. Janice handed him the purse she'd been holding.

"That belongs to her. Maybe you should take her to your place because neither Jada nor I will be home tonight."

Micah's left brow shot up. "Is that right?"

"Yup, and I know you don't want your girl to be there by herself in this condition." Janice slipped on her helmet and turned away. "Have a good night. Don't do nothin' I wouldn't do." Her laughter followed her all the way to her bike, and all Micah could do was shake his head.

Oh, this should be interesting.

He climbed into the driver's seat and glanced at his sleeping beauty. He wanted nothing more than to have Soul in his home and in his bed, but this wasn't exactly how he'd imagined it happening.

SOUL DIDN'T HAVE TO MOVE HER HEAD TO KNOW THAT IF

she did, it would probably explode. She also didn't have to open her eyes to know that Micah was nearby. His scent—a fresh, clean fragrance with a hint of sandalwood—surrounded her, lulling her back into a peaceful state, less the pounding in her head. And then there was the matter of the disgusting taste in her mouth.

What have I done?

Soul couldn't remember the last time she'd felt this bad. She wasn't much of a drinker, and if she lived through this day, she would never touch alcohol again. Bits and pieces of the night before fluttered through her mind. She vaguely recalled Micah picking her up from the bar, taking her to his home and helping her out of her clothes and into one of his T-shirts. Everything after that was a blur.

Carefully rolling onto her side, Soul slowly opened her eyes. It took blinking a few times for Micah's handsome face to come into view. He was propped up on one elbow lying next to her, looking sexier than any man had a right to look. If it weren't for feeling so crappy, she would reach out and run her fingers over the light scruff covering his cheeks and chin. She liked that he didn't shave every day, giving him a sexy, rugged look.

"I was wondering when you were going to wake up," he said. His deep, sleep-filled voice washed over her like a warm embrace, making her want to snuggle up to him.

But she didn't. Not because she didn't want to, but because she was afraid if she moved her head, it might roll off her shoulders. That's just how much it hurt.

"What do you want first—coffee or something for that headache?"

Bless him. He understood her quandary.

Soul swallowed, and the horrid taste in her mouth kept her from speaking. Then there was the nausea bubbling in her gut. Eyes drifting closed, she tried to push down the bile rising to her throat. One hand went to her stomach, and the other to her mouth.

"I don't feel so good," she mumbled, then groaned. "I think...I think I'm gonna be sick."

Micah cursed under his breath and leaped into action. He scooped her into his arms and hurried her into the bathroom. Soul barely made it to the toilet before everything she ate and drank the night before spilled from her mouth. Being this close to the porcelain goddess made her want to puke all over again.

What the heck had she been thinking last night? Who intentionally tortured their body by overdrinking only to have their face in the toilet the next morning? Worse than that, the man she wanted back in her life was seeing her at her worst.

I will never drink again. I will never drink again. The words bounced around in her mind as she emptied her stomach.

"Feel better?" Micah asked when she pushed away from the toilet and slumped against the wall. He handed her a damp washcloth, then settled on the floor next to her. The bathroom wasn't small, but his large body still consumed much of the space.

"I feel like I'm going to die."

Micah chuckled, but Soul was serious. Between the jackhammer pounding in her head, the yuckiness in her mouth, and her stomach feeling raw, it really did seem as if she was living her last days.

"What happened last night? Why all the drinking?"

Soul wiped her face and started to shake her head, but stopped when the pounding inside of her skull increased.

"I…"

What the heck could she say that wouldn't make her sound like a total loser? Feeling sorry for herself last night and trying to drown out thoughts of him suddenly seemed like a poor excuse to drink. And she was going to strangle Janice the next time she saw her. They were supposed to be friends. How could she call him? Surely, she should've known that Soul wouldn't want him to see her in this condition. It was bad enough he had to watch her spill her guts a few minutes ago. God only knew what she'd said or done last night.

"Let's just say, I had a lot on my mind. For starters, the busted pipe at the studio, water damage and dealing with an arrogant plumber. I guess I wanted to let off a little steam. Then hanging out with the girls had me reevaluating aspects of my life."

"Such as?"

"Such as things I'm not sure I'm ready to discuss yet."

Silence fell between them, and Soul didn't have to

look at Micah to know that he was staring at her. She could feel his gaze boring into her.

Instead of him pushing her to elaborate, he said, "If you change your mind, I'm here for you."

"Thank you. Actually, thank you for everything. I appreciate you picking me up last night."

"Anytime. I'm only a phone call away, but I hope the binge drinking is not going to become a habit."

"Definitely not. I'm never touching hard liquor again, and maybe not even wine. I'm pretty sure I can live on just bread and water."

"Yeah, you probably could." Micah gave her a crooked grin before standing. "I have a toothbrush on the counter for you. Along with ibuprofen, bottled water, a towel, and a T-shirt you can change into after you shower."

This man. He was so easy to love.

That's why I love you. I'll always love you.

Oh, no. Soul gripped the side of her head as she recalled saying those exact words. What else had she said or worse, what had she done?

"Do you need help showering?"

"Yes. No. I mean…"

"How about we see if you can stand up. Then you can decide if you need my help with anything."

Why did his words sound like an invitation for sex? Or maybe it was her fog-filled mind and sex-starved body wanting it to be about sex. Clearly, she needed to get laid —and soon if she was mistaking his kindness for anything more than just that.

Micah reached for her hand and pulled her up as if she weighed nothing, causing Soul to stumble into him.

"Whoa there." He captured her around the waist, but not before her hands made contact with his rock-hard abs. She hated being this close to him, knowing she probably smelled like booze and throw-up.

"I can take it from here," she murmured, gripping the edge of the vanity. He had already done more than enough for her. Glancing down at the items on the counter, Soul didn't know what to do first. Take the meds or brush her teeth. She went for the bottle of ibuprofen and took them dry, thinking she'd take a swig of water after brushing her teeth.

"I'll be in the bedroom. Holler if you need me." Micah left the bathroom, pulling the door closed but not all the way.

The lonely, in-need-of-sexual-release part of Soul wanted to call him back and invite him to shower with her, among other things. But it wouldn't be a good idea. She wanted way more from him than a quickie.

After brushing her teeth and drinking a couple of swigs of water, she stepped into the shower. Standing under the warm water, her body slowly started to relax, and the headache was now a dull thud in her skull. Now that her mind was clearer, there was one thing Soul knew for sure. She wanted Micah back in her life for good. All she had to do was figure out how to make that happen.

She rinsed the suds from her body but knocked over

the bottle of shower gel, and cringed when it noisily whacked into the glass door.

"Soul?" Micah charged into the bathroom, the door slamming into the wall. His large, powerful body was front and center. "You all right? What happened?"

"I—I dropped the…" The only thing separating them was the glass shower door, giving them both an eyeful of each other. Apparently, she had caught him in the middle of changing clothes. Micah stood before her in only a pair of boxer briefs that highlighted his huge package and tree-trunk-like thighs. A gray T-shirt dangled from his hands.

Good Lord.

When God doled out hot, sexy body parts, he had been truly generous to Micah. The man's body was absolute perfection.

While Soul's attention was on him, she had completely forgotten about her naked state. Micah's gaze traveled the length of her, and the desire gleaming in his whiskey-colored eyes couldn't be missed. Soul didn't bother trying to cover herself as his fiery gaze sent warmth surging through her body.

"Um, can you hand me that towel behind you?" she finally asked, her shaking hands fumbling with the shower faucet. Geez, he had her so worked up, it took several tries to turn off the water.

Micah didn't respond. Didn't turn away. His shirt slipped from his fingers, and he reached behind him and grabbed the towel, all without taking his eyes from her.

Instead of handing it to Soul, he held the fluffy material open.

Her heart jolted against her ribcage. This was definitely an invitation. An invitation that she willingly accepted. Without hesitation, she pushed the shower door open and stepped into his waiting arms.

Micah slowly wrapped the towel around her shivering body. He probably thought the shudder was caused by the cool air kissing her naked skin, but that wasn't the case. Her reaction had everything to do with the virile man holding her close and cradling her within his muscular embrace.

"Push me away, Soul," he mumbled gruffly as he kissed, sucked, and nibbled on her neck. "Please. Tell me to stop."

"I can't do that." He was crazy in his head if he thought she was going to push him away. "I want you. Now."

Chapter Nine

*T*he words barely rolled off of Soul's tongue before Micah crushed his mouth over hers while stripping the towel from around her body. Without breaking their kiss, his large hands gripped the back of her thighs, and he lifted her effortlessly off the floor.

This was what Soul wanted, what she needed.

Her arms went automatically around his neck, and her legs circled his waist as he backed her to the wall. The kiss was frantic, desperate, and she relished every lap of his tongue as he took full control. The beats of her heart accelerated. This was happening. This was really happening. How many times had she dreamed of being with him again?

Micah ground against her, his stiff erection confirming just how much he wanted her. Not even the rough wall at Soul's back could tamp down her need for them to be closer. Chest to chest. Skin to skin. She was more than ready to share her body with the only man she ever truly loved. Maybe she should feel self-conscious about rubbing against him, needing the friction to stimulate a part of her body that had been neglected for far too long.

"Micah, I need—"

"I know, baby," he murmured against her lips.

Holding her up with one hand, his other went to her breast, cupping it roughly before pulling the taut nipple into his mouth. Soul's mind went blank as he sucked, licked, and masterfully teased the sensitive bud. Her trembling limbs clung to him, and her nails clawed into his shoulders, trying to maintain some semblance of control. Impossible.

The erotic caress of Micah's mouth sent spirals of ecstasy charging through her body. It had been so long since she'd been with a man. So long since she experienced such an intense sexual hunger. And so long since she'd been this turned on.

Breaths came in short spurts as passion soared through Soul's body. She wanted more. She needed...

A bell sounded in the distance, but Soul blocked it out of her mind. There was nothing or nobody going to stop them from finally getting the release they both wanted. Micah wasn't detoured and didn't stop sucking on her like a man possessed.

But there it was again, some type of ringing. *The doorbell?*

Micah froze. Soul panicked.

"Baby, don't stop," she pleaded, desperation lacing her words. She was so close. Too close to stop now. "They'll go away."

Breathing hard, Micah held her tighter. He dropped his forehead to her chest and shook his head. "*Shit.* What am I doing? We can't do—"

"Yes, yes, we can. Don't stop." Soul wiggled beneath him, gripping his head and forcing him to look at her. "Ignore whoever that is. I want you, and you want me. We want this."

The tortured look in his eyes gutted her. "Not like this, sweetheart. Not before I tell…"

The doorbell rang again, and he mumbled another curse. Instead of lowering her to the floor, Micah cradled her in his arms as if she was a precious piece of china. He carried her out of the bathroom, and Soul wanted to cry. She lowered her head to his shoulder, willing herself to calm down and not take her annoyance out on him.

Without a word, he gently laid her down and pulled the covers up over her breasts. He brushed her bangs away from her eyes, looking just as miserable as she felt. If he hadn't wanted to stop, why did he? Whoever was at the door would've eventually gone away.

Micah bent down and placed a lingering kiss on her lips. "I'm sorry," he said.

Soul wasn't sure exactly what he was apologizing for. Was it because of the interruption? Was it because he stopped when she begged him not to? Or was it that he couldn't give her what she wanted, what she desired? He hesitated for a minute before moving away from the bed.

"You're not as sorry as I am," Soul grumbled under her breath, watching him slip into a pair of pants before leaving the room, closing the door behind him.

Soul flipped onto her stomach and screamed into the pillow, punching it for the interruption. Punching it for the sexual frustration clawing through her body. And she punched it because she knew that he wanted her as much as she wanted him.

THE MINUTE MICAH CLOSED THE BEDROOM DOOR, HE leaned his back against it, wondering if he had lost his mind. He had the woman of his dreams, in his arms, willing and ready to fulfill his greatest fantasy—having her again. Yet, he walked away.

In his mind and in his heart, he knew he'd done the right thing, but the rest of his body throbbed with need. The stiffy he was sporting made that abundantly clear, not caring about his moral compass. Knowing he was keeping something from her gnawed at him. Besides that, he wanted more than a quick lay from her.

Ignoring the doorbell, Micah took several deep breaths, willing his body under control. Minutes ticked by as he tried to think of anything but Soul. Anything that would get rid of his erection.

Ice shower.

Cleaning the garage.

Soul's loser ex-fiancé.

The last thought made his blood boil. Just what he needed.

The doorbell rang again.

"Who the hell can't catch a hint?"

Micah stumped to the front door. "What the heck is yo…" His voice trailed off when he swung the door open and saw who was standing on the stoop. "Mom! What are you doing here?"

"Hello to you too, dear." She pushed her long salt-and-pepper hair behind her ear as her gaze swept over his bare chest, unfastened pants, and bare feet before returning her eyes to his face. The left corner of her ruby-red lips quirked up. "Am I interrupting something? *Please*, tell me that I'm interrupting something."

Micah didn't miss the humor in her voice or the grin that spread across her mouth. She'd been on him about getting back out there and dating, and she had even fixed him up with some of her friends' daughters. Though he went out with a couple of them, he never initiated a second date. None of the women stirred anything in him. Not like with Soul. Nothing like what he felt for Soul.

"Please. Tell me that I'm interrupting something," his mother continued. "Then I'll know that I'm a little closer to getting a daughter-in-law and maybe even two or six grandkids before I die."

"Don't talk like that." Micah ran an exhausted hand over his head, feeling as if he could use a couple of more hours of sleep. "I'm pretty sure you're going to outlive everyone you know, including me."

He stepped back and let her into the house. Usually, she didn't stop by unannounced. So, whatever was in the large manila envelope she was holding in her manicured hands must've been something important.

She strolled into the living room, stylishly dressed with high-heeled sandals on, and glanced around, apparently searching for the source of his delayed response in answering the door.

"Where is she?" she asked.

Micah frowned. "Where is who?"

"The person who put those scratches on your shoulders and chest. Besides, it took you forever to come to the door, and this is the first time you've done so half-dressed."

"Did it ever occur to you that I might've worked late and was asleep?"

"No. At least not after you opened the door."

Micah sighed, knowing that she could keep this conversation going forever. "Let me go grab a shirt. Then you can tell me what's in the envelope. Feel free to get some coffee started."

He headed back to his room, not sure what he'd find. He hoped Soul was still in bed and maybe had fallen asleep, but he doubted it. She was pretty pissed when he walked out and rightfully so. He should've had more control. Shouldn't have started something he couldn't finish. But seeing her orgasm-inducing, naked body with water dripping down her dark skin had knocked all common sense from his head.

Micah pushed open the bedroom door, and Soul's head snapped up. She was sitting in bed, her back against the headboard and her knees drawn to her chest. A sheet covered her body.

He walked across the room to his dresser and pulled a white T-shirt from the top drawer, a little bothered by her silence. He'd pay money to know what she was thinking. Then again, maybe it was best he didn't know. No doubt the abrupt stop to what could've been an amazing reunion probably still bothered her as much as it bugged him. He had to fix this somehow.

After slipping into the shirt, he sat at the foot of the bed. "My mother's here, but I'll get rid of her."

"Then can you take me home?"

Crap. Disappointment vibrated through his body, and he fell back on the mattress and stared up at the two-toned tray ceiling. What the heck did he expect her to say after what happened minutes ago?

"I'll take you home…after you and I talk."

"I don't want to talk."

"*Fine.* Then you can listen," he snapped, frustration eating at him. He bolted off the bed and headed to the door, but not before he heard her call him a jackass. Yeah, he probably deserved that, considering the way he had just spoken to her.

He walked out of the room, and the moment he stepped into the hallway, the smell of coffee, bacon, and eggs permeated the air. Micah shook his head. This was quickly turning into a pain-in-the-ass morning. He should've known his mother couldn't go into the kitchen and not cook something.

He stood in the entrance to the dining room, which was connected to the kitchen and folded his arms across his chest. "What do you think you're doing?"

His mother looked up from turning the bacon. Then she flipped a couple of pancakes before responding. "What does it look like I'm doing? I'm cooking breakfast for my favorite son and his guest."

"Mom."

"Don't *mom* me. Take a look at those papers on the table and tell me if I missed anything. I want to drop them off at my lawyer's office later today."

Standing near the glass dining table, Micah pulled the document from the large envelope and quickly scanned it.

"Your will?"

"Yes. I figured it was past time I had one drawn up."

Micah appreciated her getting her life in order, but hated thinking about that she wouldn't always be around. It had been one of the hardest things he'd ever gone through when they buried his father shortly after Micah returned stateside. He couldn't imagine how hard it would be losing his mother, one of his best friends.

"Also, when you get a chance, can you…" her words trailed off as she looked at something over his shoulder.

Micah turned, surprised to see Soul dressed in the

blouse and pants that she'd had on the night before and a pair of his white socks on her small feet. When their gazes collided, his heart thudded inside his chest. She no longer looked disappointed or mad. All he saw in her eyes was love.

"Soul?" his mother gasped and shoved him out of the way to get to her. "Oh, my goodness. Is that you?"

"Yes, ma'am." Soul laughed, her face brightening at the sight of his mother. Micah was glad to see her smiling. "How are you, Ms. Pat?"

"I'm wonderful now that you're back." She threw her arms around Soul and held her tight, rocking back and forth. "Chile, I have missed you something terrible. Let me look at you." She pulled back without releasing Soul. "You're still the prettiest little thing."

Soul smiled shyly, and Micah's heart rattled inside his chest. Having her in his home, talking to his mother felt surreal. Like she…like they were right where they were supposed to be. If it took him the rest of his life, he planned to make her his again.

"Are you here just for a visit? Or are you…" She looked between Micah and Soul. "Are you two back together?"

Soul's eyes grew round, and she glanced at Micah. "Uh, I—"

"Mom, like you always tell me. Stay out of grown folks' business."

She plopped her hands on her round hips and glared at him. "I'm your mother."

"Yeah, and I'm grown. When Soul and I are ready to tell you anything, we'll…tell you. In the meantime, don't you have somewhere to be?"

She *tsk*ed and waved him off and turned back to Soul. "Next Friday night I'm having an all-white party for my birthday, and I want you there. You can even bring him…" she nodded toward Micah, "…if you want."

Soul burst out laughing. "I have so missed you. You haven't changed a bit," she said to his mother. "I'd love to attend your party. Just give me the time and the place. I'll be there."

Micah shoved his hands into his pants pockets. *This little visit is turning out better than I could've planned.*

Chapter Ten

*A*fter cleaning up the breakfast dishes, Soul poured herself another cup of coffee while Micah walked his mother to her car. She carried the large mug to the counter next to the window and sat on one of the barstools.

Micah had a nice home. Soul had given herself a quick tour of his three-bedroom, two-bathroom bungalow before greeting his mother earlier. The house had been purchased a couple of years ago, and it was definitely a bachelor's pad. Minimum furnishings, plain white walls with no pictures hanging on them, and humongous televisions in his bedroom and the living room made up the decor.

Bringing the steaming cup of coffee to her mouth, Soul stared out the window at the gurgling fountain near the array of rose bushes lining the back fence. Her mind took her immediately back to the little tryst in the bathroom. No longer pissed at Micah, she still couldn't help wondering why he had stopped. She practically begged him to take everything she was willing to give, and she knew he was interested. Yet, he deprived them both from having a morning they wouldn't soon forget between the sheets. Or against a bathroom wall.

Her lips twitched, and she fought back a smile. Hot, sweaty sex in a bathroom would've been a first for her. Since Micah had been her first...everything, she would've loved to add another first with him.

"You ready to talk?"

Soul startled and turned to find him a few feet away. Now that his mother wasn't there, things felt a little awkward. He was right, they did need to talk.

He strolled across the kitchen to one of the cabinets, and Soul's gaze went immediately to his tight butt. His perfectly round, tight butt that made her want to reach out and squeeze it.

"Here's a travel mug you can use if you prefer we talk while I drive you home," he said as he turned, but stopped abruptly and narrowed his eyes. "Were you staring at my butt?"

"Yeah. Couldn't help myself," she said honestly. No sense in lying.

He flashed his wicked crooked grin and heat spread through her body. This man. This sweet, strong, hand-some man was seeping deeper and deeper into her heart. With just a smile, he made her pulse race, and Soul wasn't sure what she'd do if they couldn't get their relationship on track. Whatever burden he was carrying that kept him from claiming her as his own must be pretty heavy.

"Thanks for the mug, but maybe we can talk here."

"I think that's a good idea. Let's take this into the living room," he said, reaching for her coffee. Soul followed him into the cozy room where the white brick fireplace was the focal point. He nodded for her to have a seat on the black leather sofa while he set her coffee on one of the side tables near her.

The first few minutes, they sat in silence. He was on the sofa, too, but kept a little distance between them, which she hated. As a matter of fact, the whole time his mother had been there, Micah barely touched her. Though each time she looked up, he was watching her.

She wasn't sure how to broach the subject of that morning. Maybe it was good his mother showed up when she had. The last thing Soul wanted was for Micah to have any regrets whenever they did finally make love.

"About this morning."

"I love your mom."

They both spoke at the same time, then laughed.

"You go first," Soul said.

He reached over and grasped her hand. "I'm sorry things went a little too far this morning. But don't think that I don't want you. Hell, I crave you, Soul."

"Then why'd you stop? Why do I feel like there's some invisible barrier wedged between us that you can't get past?"

He released a long, drawn-out sigh and squeezed her hand. Resting his head against the back of the sofa, he stared straight ahead. Just when she thought he wouldn't respond, he said, "Unlike years ago, I play for keeps, Soul. I've made it no secret how I feel about you, but I still want marriage. I still want children. I can't start something with you when I know we don't want the same thing."

"But we do want the same thing. I told you that." He still had ahold of her hand and Soul moved closer to him, deciding to speak from the heart. "I'm not going to lie. The thought of having a child or children and suffering the same fate as my mother is never far from my mind. Years ago, when we had this conversation, I was young and naïve. I honestly didn't think I could handle marriage when I knew I had no intention of having children.

"But Micah, you're still in my heart. Spending the last couple of weeks with you has only intensified how much I care about you. I want you in my life…for good. I want what you want. Together we can accomplish anything, including helping me get past my fears. Please don't give up on me. Not this time."

Micah didn't respond, but he brought her hand to his mouth and kissed the back of her fingers. Staring at her, he searched her eyes. Soul wasn't exactly sure what he was looking for but hoped he knew she meant every word she'd just spoken.

"I say we give us another chance, but I want us to wait regarding consummating our relationship."

Soul tried to school her face to look disappointed, but she couldn't stop the smile from peeking through. "Well, that kind of sucks. However, since we're officially dating, and you're mine, I guess I can wait until you're ready."

He laughed and pulled her into his arms. "Talk about role reversal," he said, nibbling on her top lip and then her bottom one. It was role reversal indeed. When they were younger, he'd been ready to take their relationship to the next level before she'd been. He had given her a similar speech about being willing to wait until she was ready.

Soul's phone, which lay on the dining room table, rang. At first, she thought about letting it go to voicemail but then changed her mind.

"I should get that. It's probably Jada or Janice calling to check on me." She hurried out of the room, sliding a little bit across the hardwood floors in Micah's socks. By the time she picked up the device, it had stopped ringing.

"Oh well. I tried," she murmured to herself.

Seconds later, the phone chirped with a voice message.

"Hello, Soul."

Soul's body stiffened at the sound of Ryan's voice, and she wondered why he was calling her.

"I know you're surprised to hear from me, but you're never far from my thoughts. I need to talk to you. I need to explain a few things, but I'll call you back."

Soul glanced at the recent call log. The number was unknown. When she hit the "call" button, it just rang.

"You okay?"

Soul jumped at Micah's voice. For a big guy, he moved around soundlessly. His hand settled on her hip, and he gave her a little squeeze.

"You all right? Who was on the phone?"

"It was Ryan. I can't believe he called."

Micah's hand stilled. "What did the bastard want?" There was a hardness in his tone that wasn't there minutes ago. Soul didn't know what his problem was with Ryan. It wasn't like they knew each other.

Micah stepped away from her and ran his hand over his mouth. He wasn't glaring anymore, the intense vibe bouncing off of him made it clear he was struggling to keep his attitude in check. No matter how many times she told him that she was over Ryan, he still got a little uptight whenever she mentioned his name.

"He didn't say much, and the call was static-y."

"If he calls again, I want to know. I don't care when, what time of day, or where I'm at, call me."

Confused, Soul shook her head, trying to make sense of his attitude. "Micah, Ryan calling means nothing. I'm with you now." She squeezed his arm. "He's not the man I want. You are. Only you. No one else."

He pulled out one of the dining room chairs and dropped down in it with a huff. "I—I know, and I'm sorry. Hell, it seems like I've been apologizing a lot lately. I didn't mean to snap. It's just—"

"It's just you're jealous." Soul laughed, and warmth spread through her body.

"I'm not jealous," he insisted. "Okay, maybe a little. I don't want him anywhere near you. Heck, I don't even want him calling you."

Soul couldn't wipe the smile off her face. She had never had a man to be jealous over her, and she kind of liked how it felt. Moving closer to him, she straddled his lap, knowing she was entering dangerous territory. She planned to respect his request that they take things slow, but she had no intention of making it easy for him.

Wrapping her arms around his neck, she kissed him sweetly, hoping to wipe away any doubts he might have about them or her and Ryan. If anyone would have told her months ago when she moved to Atlanta that she would reconnect with her college sweetheart, she would've laughed in their face. Even though she fantasized about them one day getting back together, she never imagined that it could actually happen.

She lifted her head and framed Micah's face between her hands as she stared into his magnificent brown eyes. "I'm yours, and nothing or no one will ever come between us again."

"I'm going to hold you to that," he said before claiming her mouth.

Oh yeah, she was going to love being his woman again.

❄

Days later, Micah drove through the dark streets of East Atlanta in his squad car, still stressing over the fact that Ryan had reached out to Soul. As far as he knew, the guy had only called that one time, but Micah still didn't like it. Myles had assured him that they still had eyes on Soul's ex and that he hadn't left Dallas. If only the Feds would go ahead and pick him up, get the guy off the streets, and put an end to the whole situation.

"This has been a long-ass night," Caden Burrell, Micah's partner of four years, said from the passenger seat.

He was right. The evening had been more active than usual. They had already responded to a couple of suspicious person activity calls, some disturbances, a collision, and they had just received a tip that a guy they'd been looking for had been spotted.

Micah turned right at the next corner and slowed. The sun had set, but streaks of orange, yellow, and purple hues still painted the sky, offering the usually dark roads in that part of town additional light. The extra light was helpful since the few streetlamps barely illuminated the area.

As they crept down the street, a few teens hung out on the sidewalk, while others took up space on their porches. Despite how crazy the evening had been, the weather had cooled to a comfortable temperature for an Atlanta summer night.

"Wait. Slow down," Caden said, his focus on the house a few doors down where Vondale Davis's woman lived. They had a warrant for his arrest and had been searching for him a couple of days.

"You actually think he's just going to be hanging out waiting for us to pick him up?" Micah asked.

"Yep, 'cause you know he only comes out after dark."

Which was the main reason they were creeping around his woman's neighborhood. Micah stopped and parked the car two doors down from the house.

"You know how sneaky he is. You take the front, and I'll go around to the back," Caden said as they crossed the street.

"Sounds good."

Pop! Pop!

Micah and Caden flinched, immediately reaching for their weapons at the burst of gunshots that rang out. The kids who were on the sidewalk scattered in the opposite direction when there was another shot. Micah ducked behind a tree and called for backup.

Why, that little...

Vondale darted across a front lawn before ducking between two houses, and Micah took off after him. Caden went in a different direction to cut him off.

"Stop! Police!" Micah yelled when Vondale hustled toward a back fence and leaped, barely clearing the wooden plank. Micah cursed and followed.

I'm getting too old for this crap. Each time he had to chase down some lowlife for doing stupid shit, he considered giving up the badge and changing careers.

"Stop! Police!" He cut across two backyards, sidestepping a tricycle and a skateboard as he shortened the distance between them. Vondale grabbed onto another fence, ready to catapult over it. Just as he swung his right foot up, Micah grabbed the back of the guy's shirt.

"Get down from there!" One good yank and Vondale tumbled to the ground. "Stay down." Micah tackled him, planting his knee in the center of his back until he could holster his gun. Then he cuffed him.

"Come on, bro. You know you can let me go."

"Man, aren't you getting tired of this life? Your ass is twenty-four years old. You know better than to—"

"Just get off me! I didn't do nothin'."

"Then why'd you run?" Micah asked while he searched Vondale for a weapon, ultimately pulling a pistol from the scum's waistband. "And you're carrying a concealed weapon. You're under arrest."

Vondale wiggled around on the ground until Micah hauled him to his feet. He shoved him against the chain-link fence.

"Damn, man. Get off me!" Vondale looked around, his eyes wild as if high on something. "Help! Police brutality! Somebody help!"

"Shut up." Micah turned him around to face the fence and tightened his hold. "You got any needles in your pockets?" he asked, continuing the pat down with his free hand.

"Nah, man. I don't do drugs."

"Yeah, right." Micah carefully pulled a canvas wallet from Vondale's back pocket and flipped it open. He glanced at the ID and contents before returning the thread-frayed billfold to the kid's pocket. After finding some coins, a pack of gum, and a dime bag, he swung Vondale around to face him.

Micah held up the weed. "Don't do drugs, huh?"

"That's not mine."

"Yeah, tell it to the judge. Let's go."

"Get off me." Vondale jerked his body back and forth, kicking out his legs and trying to get loose. "I ain't doin' nothin'. Let me go."

"Looks like I'll be adding resisting arrest to your charges."

"You got nothin' on me, man." Vondale slammed his head into Micah's face.

A stab of pain shot through his jaw and stole his breath. "Damn it!" Micah clenched his teeth at the fiery sensation just under his right eye. Before he could stop himself, he slammed Vondale hard against the fence. Anger clawed through his body. "I ought to…"

Caden rounded the house, breathing hard with another perp in handcuffs, and Micah cursed again. That anger from moments ago quickly turned to fear at what he might've done to Vondale if Caden hadn't shown up.

Damn. That was close. Too close.

Chapter Eleven

*S*oul woke with a start and bolted upright. Pulse pounding loudly in her ear, she glanced around the family room, trying to figure out what had awakened her. The lights were off, and the room was lit only by the television screen, but nothing seemed out of place.

That's when she heard it. Banging on the wall.

Her gaze went to the ceiling, wondering what Jada was doing up there. Again, there was a steady *thump... thump...thump* that slowly increased in speed.

What the...

Passionate moans and groans ricocheted off the walls and drifted down to Soul's ears. Her mouth gaped open as the sounds grew louder and louder and...

"Oh. My. God. Are you frickin' kidding me right now?" she ground out and dropped her head back on the sofa, and covered her ears with two pillows.

Please let them get this over with soon.

Apparently, Solomon had stayed the night. Soul had no idea the walls were that thin. She might've been glad her friend was getting some, but she preferred not hearing every squeak, moan, and whimper coming from upstairs. Especially when she hadn't had a little somethin'-somethin' in, like, forever.

That thought had her sitting up again and tossing the pillows to the side. Placing her feet on the floor, she reached for her cell phone that was on the coffee table and glanced at the screen. Still no call. It was just after midnight and Micah hadn't checked in with her. Which was odd. Usually, even when he worked a double, they talked a couple of times a day.

"Actually…" Soul called his cell, thinking he should've gotten off an hour ago. Why hadn't he called to at least say goodnight? That was something he had started doing even before they officially started dating the other day.

When the voicemail picked up, she left a message.

"Hey, babe. Just checking on you. Give me a call as soon as you get this message." After hanging up, she sent him a quick text, hoping that he was okay. Soul had always been a worrier but hadn't had anyone special in her life to worry about in a long time.

She smiled at the thought, but it was short-lived when the thumping above her head grew even louder. Then faster. And then…a passionate scream pierced the quietness of the room, and she cringed.

"Ugh! I just can't."

She leaped off the sofa and headed to the kitchen, trying to wipe her mind free of the visual that those sounds had created. She shuddered at the thought. Who knew Jada was a screamer?

From now on, whenever Solomon stayed over, Soul would have to make sure she camped out in another part of the house. Or better yet, maybe with Micah.

Determined to stay up until she heard from him, she made herself a cup of coffee and popped some popcorn. Hoping that Jada and Solomon were done screwing around for the night, she went back to the family room and curled up on the sofa. She wasn't much of a TV watcher, but tonight she'd binge out on whatever show she ran across.

Looking at her phone again, disappointment lodged in her chest when Micah still hadn't responded. Soul texted him again as worry started creeping in.

I'm trying not to worry, but I need to hear from you ASAP.

Picking up the television remote, she scrolled through channels and stopped when she found one of her favorite movies, *Pretty Woman*. It didn't matter how many times she watched it, she still laughed at the same parts.

"You're on my fax."

"Well, that's one I haven't been on before."

Stuffing popcorn into her mouth, she lost track of time as she recited practically every line of the chick flick.

And toward the end of the movie, she got teary-eyed when Vivian said her goodbyes at the hotel.

This world could use more romantic comedies, Soul thought when the credits started rolling. She lifted her arms high above her head and stretched. It had been a long day, and she was pretty sure her body would be screaming at her in the morning for sitting around for hours.

Yawning loudly, she glanced at her phone again. No call. At first, she was worried, now she was just pissed. She and Micah were going to have a long talk and nail down protocols for days he worked late.

Footsteps on the stairs caught Soul's attention.

"Who's there," she called out, hoping it wasn't Jada or Solomon. Seeing either of them anytime soon would just be too weird.

Janice pushed her hot pink glasses up on her nose as she stood in the doorway. The woman had more eyewear, and in every color, than anyone Soul knew.

"I'm surprised you're still up. You're usually in bed before the streetlights come on," she said.

Soul threw the last popcorn kernel at her. "Ha, ha. Very funny." She might not be a night owl, but she wasn't that bad. "I've been waiting for Micah to call, but maybe I should call it a night. What about you? It's almost one-thirty in the morning. Where are you off to?"

"I need to go handle some grown-folks business." She wiggled her brows, causing her glasses to slide down her nose. "See you tomorrow. Oh, wait. It is tomorrow. I guess I'll see you later."

Soul shook her head as her friend bounded out of the house. She was pretty sure grown-folks business meant booty-call. At least her friends were getting their needs met, she thought as she picked up the television remote to scroll through the channels again. Stopping on a news station, something she rarely watched, she glanced at the words scrolling across the bottom.

Breaking News: Police involved shooting in East Point. One officer killed after responding to a disturbance. Two people wounded, including the suspect, who is in custody.

Oh God. Soul dropped the remote as panic clawed through her while the words scrolled across the bottom of the screen again.

Please, please, please, don't let it be him.

Two hours later, Soul still hadn't heard from Micah, and she was a nervous wreck. She swiped at her eyes, fighting the tears that wouldn't stop falling. At first, she tried convincing herself that it wasn't him. That he couldn't be gone, but...

"It's him. I'm afraid it's him," she whispered, trying to hold herself together. "Otherwise, he would've been home when I went by there, or he would've called me by now. Jada, he always calls."

"I know, sweetie, and he still will." Jada stood leaning against a wall in the hallway where Soul was pacing. She had come downstairs an hour ago for water, shortly after Soul had returned from Micah's house.

If only he had been home.

"Did you call Myles? Maybe he's heard from Micah or can get in touch with him."

"I left a voicemail, but I don't expect to hear from him. He's been on some type of secret assignment at work, and I don't even know if he has his phone on him."

"According to the news, it seemed like there's been a lot going on tonight," Jada said on a yawn. "You don't even know if he was in that area at the time of the shooting."

"That's just it. I don't know anything. I don't know what precinct he works out of. I don't know who to call when something like this happens or what to do. I don't even know his mother's telephone number." She probably wouldn't have called Ms. Pat anyway, just in case Micah wasn't the one who'd been killed.

"He's probably so busy and not thinking that you might've seen the news. Now come and sit down. You're going to make yourself sick."

Feeling drained, Soul lumbered back into the family room with leaden feet dragging her down. She was at a loss of who else to call or what to do and losing hope fast.

"I can't do this. Police officers put their lives at risk every day," she said when Jada sat on the sofa next to her. "There's too much craziness in this city. I'll never be able to sleep or have any peace knowing Micah is out there on those streets. I don't think I can handle dating a cop."

Chapter Twelve

*M*icah rang the doorbell again, hating to be stopping by in the middle of the morning, but he needed to see Soul. This had been one of the longest nights of his career. A night full of more bloodshed than he'd seen on this side of the world. Things had been so out of control, especially after one of their own was killed, that Micah hadn't realized he had lost his phone.

But even if Myles hadn't called the precinct and left a message and his number, Micah had planned to stop by Soul's place. He needed to be with her, someone who reminded him that there was good and sweetness in the world.

He started to ring the doorbell again, but the door swung open. Jada stood there for a full minute, looking him up and down before she spoke.

"You'd better have a good reason for scaring her half to death tonight."

She opened the door wider and stepped back, and Micah's gaze landed on Soul, who was a few feet away. His heart thudded in his chest. She looked so small and fragile, and her eyes were red and swollen.

Jada squeezed his arm and pulled him inside the house. "I'm glad you're okay, but you better fix this."

She walked away without another word, and Soul eased forward. Her gaze frantically traveled the length of him before her attention returned to his face. "You're hurt," she said, biting her bottom lip as tears filled her eyes.

Micah had temporarily forgotten about the bruise on his face from when Vondale headbutted him. "I'm all right. Just a little incident earlier tonight, but I'm okay." At the moment, he itched to hold her. Kiss her. Soak up her warmth. He reached for her, and she lunged into his arms and then burst into tears.

"Aw, baby. I'm so sorry. I didn't mean to scare you."

Her arms tightened around his neck as she sobbed, and Micah's heart cracked a little. He never wanted to do anything that would hurt her, even unintentionally. Jada was right. He needed to fix this.

He continued to hold Soul, probably a little too tight, but he couldn't help it. He needed her. Needed to have her close. The way he was feeling, he might not ever let her go. "Shh, it's okay. I'm okay."

"I love you." Her voice was muffled against his neck. "I thought I lost you."

There had been several times during the night that he'd wanted to text her to give a shout out or call to hear her voice. There just hadn't been time. Then when he realized he had lost his phone, including all the numbers he didn't know by heart, it was at the end of his shift. The moment Myles reamed him out for being off the radar and for scaring Soul, Micah headed right to her.

Dead on his feet, he lowered Soul to the floor. He needed some sleep but knew that wouldn't happen without having her in his arms. "I know we need to talk, but not right now. Right now, all I want to do is hold you in my arms so that we both can get some sleep."

Soul nodded. "I'd like that. Do you want to come upstairs?"

"No. I want you to go upstairs and pack a bag. You're coming home with me."

An hour later, Micah finally crawled into bed next to Soul. Marveling at how perfect she looked in his bed. She had fallen asleep the moment her head hit the pillow, and he couldn't much blame her. It was almost four in the morning, and if given a chance, he could sleep for a week. But before he switched off the bedside lamp, he just wanted to look at his beautiful woman. Not knowing if he was dead or alive had really done a number on her, and Micah never wanted to put her through that again.

He turned off the light. Wrapping his arms around Soul, he held her close and inhaled the scent that was uniquely her. What would it be like to fall asleep with her in his arms every night? That was his last thought before drifting off to sleep.

When Soul woke up, her head was nestled against Micah's chest, and part of her body was sprawled over his. He felt so good beneath her that she never wanted to move from that spot. The only problem was, his arm around her was like being trapped in the jaws of a vise grip. Yet, she didn't want to wake him, knowing he was tired after the day he'd had yesterday.

Barely able to see over his body, she glanced at the clock on the nightstand. *Twelve-thirty.*

Soul dropped her head back onto Micah's chest as memories of the night before flashed across her mind. If that ordeal revealed nothing else, it reminded her of how precious life was and how she couldn't take anything for granted. Especially Micah. If there was any doubt in her mind that she didn't love him, that was squashed hours ago. Not only did she love him, but she didn't want to live without him in her life.

On the way to his house, Micah had promised that in the future, if word got out that an officer was down, he'd find a way to let her know that he was all right. He also planned to give her all of his contact information, including the precinct's number and his boss's number, as well as his mother's info.

Soul was satisfied with that but was still anxious about dating a cop. She hadn't shared that with Micah and wasn't sure when she would.

"Good morning," he said in a deep rasp and shook her a little as if to get her attention.

Soul glanced up at him. He still looked a little tired, but she was glad to be there with him.

"Good morning. I hope I didn't wake you."

"You didn't. Did you sleep okay?"

She nodded and slid up his body with the intent to get closer to his mouth, but accidentally rubbed up against his morning woody.

He moaned, and his large hands gripped her hips, moving her up and down against his length. "God, you feel good," he murmured, nipping at the sensitive spot below her ear.

The heat Micah generated by rubbing against her sex was almost unbearable. It didn't matter that she was wearing panties and he was in his boxer briefs. Soul could feel all of him, and she wanted to have him buried deep inside of her.

She straddled his hips and boldly ground against him, loving the erotic sounds he was making as she rotated her hips.

"Aw, baby. You're starting something that I'm definitely going to have to finish."

Soul leaned down and kissed him. "Good, because the only way we're stopping this time is for you to grab a condom."

"I can do that, but first I need you out of this T-shirt."

Micah didn't wait for her to take it off. He slid his hands beneath the hem, and his scorching touch on her skin sent electric currents shooting through her body. The shirt was removed in an instant, leaving her breasts bare for him to feast on.

"Damn, you have a beautiful body."

He pulled her forward and cupped one of her breasts before his mouth covered her perky nipple. Soul's eyes drifted closed, and she moaned at the heady sensation stirring inside of her with every lap of his tongue. The lower part of her body moved on its own accord, grinding against his shaft as his tongue swirled around her nipple. When Micah paid the same homage to her other breasts, she knew she couldn't take much more.

"I need to be inside of you now," he said.

Soul gasped, totally caught off guard when he flipped her onto her back in one smooth motion. Then she laughed. "In a hurry, are we?"

"Yeah, 'cause you do something to me that tests what little self-control I have. Now, let's get you naked."

Within seconds, they had stripped down, and Soul had the pleasure of seeing all of him. He looked amazing in clothes, but she had never seen a more beautiful sight than him without anything on.

The left corner of his mouth quirked up as she checked him out. Clearly, he was comfortable in his skin and rightfully so. The man's body was sheer perfection.

When he reached over to the nightstand to retrieve a condom, Soul couldn't help herself. She fisted her hand over his shaft, and he practically leaped off the bed.

"Baby, if you grip me that tight, this will be over way before we start."

Soul didn't release him, but pumped her hand up and down his length, and circled the tip with the pad of her thumb. With each passionate sound he made, she increased the speed and the pressure.

"Okay. Okay."

Micah eased her hand away, then quickly sheathed himself. As he lowered his mouth to hers, kissing her tenderly, he nudged her thighs apart. Soul's heart thumped wildly against her chest, and she gripped his thighs, digging her nails into him as he slid into her heat.

"Relax, baby. Look at me," Micah crooned. She did as he commanded and saw such love and passion sparkling in his eyes. The moment Soul relaxed her interior muscles, he started moving inside of her. Slowly at first, but quickly picking up speed. With each thrust, she rotated her hips, matching him stroke for stroke as he went deeper and harder.

It had been so long since they'd been together, but it was as if their bodies were in tune to each other. Moving as one. Hitting each note together. Soul's desire was that they'd find their way back to one another in every way possible, but being with him like this again was better than ever. Every nerve in her body was alive as her pulse raced, and she neared her release.

With one last thrust, wave after wave of pleasure shot through Soul's body, stealing her breath as her orgasm rocked her to the core. Even while she gasped for air, Micah kept pumping in and out of her until his explosive release soon followed.

He collapsed on top of her, but lifted slightly, bracing himself to keep from putting all of his weight on her.

"Man," was all he said before his lips slowly met hers.

Micah kissed her with a passion that was so raw, but tender. And something so magical passed between them. Soul couldn't put a name to it. All she could do was savor the moment.

When the kiss ended and Micah lifted his head, he stared into her eyes. "I love you. I love you so much," he said with such heartfelt emotion, and Soul's heart sang.

She cupped his cheek and brushed her thumb over the scruff on his face. "I love you even more."

It was a miracle that they'd found their way back to each other, and Soul looked forward to seeing what the future held.

MICAH SIGHED CONTENTLY AS HE LAY WITH SOUL snuggled up against him. Two rounds of sex with her weren't nearly enough, but they both were still a little tired from the night before. They had always been perfect together, but the last couple of hours were like a dream come true. This was what he wanted. Her. In his life. In his bed. Forever.

But as he stared down at her sleeping form, guilt slashed through him. He'd had no intention of taking their relationship to the next level. At least not before telling her about Ryan. Each time Micah considered sharing what was going on, something stopped him. Fear of losing her? Or maybe it was fear of her walking away without looking back.

He knew Soul well enough to know that when she found out, she'd be pissed at Myles, but as for Micah, she'd be disappointed. They had always been honest with each other, and he didn't want their second chance at love to be any different.

I have to tell her…soon.

Chapter Thirteen

*M*icah pulled up to Club Masquerade, one of the hottest night clubs in the city, and fell in line behind other vehicles to have his truck valeted. His mother never did things halfway. For her sixty-fifth birthday, she had reserved one of the club's VIP sections.

Micah glanced at Soul sitting in the passenger seat. Checking her out while she glanced out the window at the crowd lining up to get into the club. He and Soul were dressed in all white as per his mother's request, but Soul's outfit took his breath away.

The dress was backless, as well as low cut, and highlighted every delicious curve of her body. The daring outfit had a silver beaded strap that went around her neck, holding up the top half of the dress. Large cutouts on the sides showed smooth, dark skin and a narrow waist. The bottom half of the dress flowed over her body like a second skin and stopped just below her knees.

But it was the jaw-dropping, side split up the left leg that was going to cause problems tonight. Micah could barely keep his eyes off of her. No doubt other men would have the same problem, too. The split showed way too much of her shapely thigh and gave a peek at her hip with every step she took.

"I'm not sure how I feel about you wearing this dress," he said as he helped her out of the truck. "I'm telling you now. If any man looks at you wrong, I'm taking him out back and beat his ass."

Soul burst out laughing. "Oh, my goodness. You've been hanging out with Myles too long. That sounds like something he would say. Actually, it also sounds like something he would do." Soul reached for his hand and flashed him a sweet smile, one that Micah wanted to see on her pretty face at all times. "But don't worry. I'm yours, and you're the one I'm going home with tonight."

Now Micah was the one smiling. He stopped in the middle of the sidewalk and kissed her hard. "I love it when you talk like that. I say we give this party a couple of hours and then get out of here."

"We'll see. Let's go in before your mother calls again. She already told me that if you changed your mind about coming, to leave you and come anyway."

Micah chuckled. "I always knew she loved you more than me."

An hour into the festivities and Micah was ready to leave. He had spent the better part of his time dancing with his woman, but unlike him, Soul could dance all night. Now he was on the second level of the club, near the VIP section, sipping a glass of whiskey as he bobbed his head to the latest song by Khalid.

The DJ was on point, playing everything from Motown classics to rap. The evening was in full swing with club hoppers and party-goers mingling, drinking, and having a good time.

Leaning on the railing, Micah glanced down at the dance floor. His mother, her friends, and Soul had danced to practically every song. But it was Soul who made every nerve in his body come alive.

Entranced by that sexy dress, and how her graceful movements made her stand out from the rest, Micah watched as she broke off from the others and started dancing alone. She looked as if she had mentally blocked out everyone else and was caught up in her own little world. Strong and willowy, her limbs moved with fluidity, becoming one with the music.

"Myles mentioned that Soul was back in town. I see she can still command attention when she dances," Mason Bennett, one of the club's owners, said when he walked up to Micah. Mase, as most people called him, was also the owner of Supreme Security-Atlanta and a fellow Marine vet.

"Yeah, she commands attention on and off the dance floor," Micah said, chuckling while shaking Mason's hand. They had met on several occasions over the years. The club was in Micah's patrol area, and he had responded a few times when fights broke out. "It's good seeing you again."

"Yeah, you too. How've you been?" Mason asked.

"Not bad, and you?"

"I'm all right." Mason swirled the dark liquid in his glass then took a sip. "Have you thought any more about joining my team of security specialists?"

Micah nodded. "More often than not lately," he said.

After the night that Soul thought he'd been killed, Micah had really started thinking about changing careers. As a security specialist, the job could still be dangerous, but not like being a cop where he put his life on the line every day.

Mason reached in the inside pocket of his black suit jacket and pulled out a business card. "Well, give me a call when you're ready. We'd love to have you on our team."

"I'll do that." Micah pocketed the card and returned his attention to Soul. She hadn't asked him to leave the force, but whenever he discussed his job, her anxiousness was palpable. A change like this would be good for them, and it would show her that he was serious about having a future with her.

When the song ended, those who had stood back to watch Soul dance clapped and whistled. She looked a little shell-shocked at first, as if not realizing people had been watching, but smiled and gave a slight bow.

Micah was so impressed by her humbleness. A world-class dancer, gracing the dance floor in a night club, was a big deal. Yet, she didn't see it like that. She saw herself as just another person who loved to dance.

When the DJ slowed the music down, playing "A Quiet Time to Play," an oldie by Johnny Gill, Micah took it as a cue to go and dance with his woman. He handed his empty glass to a server passing by, and then made his way down the stairs.

Soul was standing a few feet from the dance floor near the illuminated glass bar, wiping her forehead with a napkin. Micah couldn't wait to have her body hugged up to his. But as he moved closer, panic rioted through his body when a tall man with a low fade, and similar height and build as her ex-fiancé approached her. Micah had seen numerous photos of Ryan, and from a distance, it looked like him.

With his heart racing, he shoved past people. Stepped on toes. And kept moving toward the bar. As he neared, Micah saw the guy gripping Soul's elbow and pointing to the dance floor. Despite her shaking her head *no*, he was still trying to pull her out there.

To anyone else, it might've looked as if he was just asking her to dance, but Micah saw the wariness in Soul's eyes and the firm set of her mouth. She was nervous, or maybe even scared.

"Oh, come on, sweetness. You can teach me a few moves, and I can show you what I'm working with."

Anger charged through Micah with a vengeance, and he snatched the guy by the back of his collar. Jerking him away from her, he wrapped his hand around the man's neck. "What part of *no* don't you understand? If you put your hands on her again——"

"Man, get off of me." The man batted Micah's hand away, and Micah charged at him again, grabbing hold of his shirt.

Two security guys came out of nowhere. "All right, that's enough," one of them said. They got between Micah and the other man, pushing them both in opposite directions.

The one holding Micah loosened his grip and said, "Mase told me to tell you that either you chill out, or he's calling the cops."

Micah rubbed the back of his neck and laughed. It was nice to know Mason had a sense of humor. "Tell him that won't be necessary."

Once security walked away, Micah turned and found Soul staring at him, her mouth gaping open as he approached her.

"You okay?" he asked, swallowing hard at the thought that he'd been too far away from her. What if that had been Ryan? Her ex could've easily tossed her little self over his shoulder and carried her out of the building.

"Don't you think you were a little rough with the guy?" she asked, slipping her hand into his.

"No. I don't. Now dance with me." Micah guided her to the dance floor, then pulled her into his arms. "I told you what I was going to do if a man looked at you wrong."

Soul leaned her head back. "I'm going to have to keep you away from my brother."

The mention of Myles stirred that guilt that already swirling inside of Micah. He was definitely going to have to come clean, and sooner than later.

Chapter Fourteen

Standing in his kitchen, Micah poured himself a glass of water, still thinking about the incident on the dance floor. He should've been embarrassed by his behavior, but he wasn't. The thought of any man pushing up on Soul the way that guy had made his blood boil. It didn't help that Micah initially thought it could've been Ryan.

"What's wrong?" Soul asked when she strolled into the kitchen. She had changed out of her dress and into a fitted T-shirt and lounging pants.

"What do you mean?"

"I mean something has been bothering you since we left the party. You're not still thinking about that guy, are you?"

Micah hesitated before speaking, conflicting thoughts warring inside his mind. Soul was giving him the perfect opportunity to tell her about Ryan, and he wasn't sure he was ready. Her life might not be in danger. Myles could be overreacting. But still, Micah felt she had a right to know what Myles had done, and that her ex was under investigation.

"There's something I need to tell you. Come and have a seat." Micah pulled out one of the dining room chairs for her and then sat in the one to her right. "It's about Ryan."

Soul sat up straighter. "What about him? And please don't tell me that you're still tripping over that phone call. It was one time, Micah. I've only heard from him once."

He sighed and pinched the bridge of his nose. "It's not that. It's…" Usually, he didn't have a problem saying what was on his mind, but with Soul, it was different. He never wanted to do anything to upset or disappoint her.

"It's what? Micah, you're scaring me. Did something happen? Is Ryan hurt?"

The last question shook something loose inside of him. Something that made him want to blurt out that the guy was a loser and had been no good for her. How could she still be concerned about a man who had wronged her?

"No, he's under investigation for money laundering," Micah bit out, trying to tap down his frustration. "He works for a known gun smuggler. We're not sure about Ryan, but we know the man he works for, Ebolsa, is a very dangerous man."

Her brows dipped into a frown. "What? That's crazy. There's no way he's involved in anything like that. Ryan is a laid-back guy who watches too much TV, lives on junk food, and wouldn't even kill a fly. He would never get involved with someone who deals with guns. He's an accountant, for Christ's sake."

"The FBI has eyes on him, Soul. Which is why Myles and I are concerned that you might end up being collateral damage if things go sideways for him."

She shook her head and stood, folding her arms across her chest as confusion showed on her face. "What does that even mean? And how are you involved in any of this? Do you know Ryan?"

Micah stood, too, and ran his hand over his head and let it slide to the back of his neck. Tension was slowly seeping in. "I never met him, but Myles filled me in on his dealings. He asked me to stay close and keep an eye on you just in case Ryan made an appearance."

"Why would he make an appearance?"

"Because he loved you, Soul!"

"He dumped me and moved to God knows where. I…" Her words trailed off, and her frown shifted. Her brows lifted and she stepped away from him as if suddenly realizing something. "If what you're saying is true…if he really was in love with me, why did he leave? Why did he suddenly break off our engagement?"

Dread filled Micah. Having this conversation was starting to feel like a bad idea. He should've just continued letting the guilt gnaw at him. It would've been better than having to tell her everything.

"Tell me!" she shouted as if already knowing the answer.

"Myles made him walk away."

Soul covered her face with her hands and released a loud, agonizing growl. Then she dropped her arms and laughed. Not a *that's funny* type of laugh, but one that lacked humor. A dry, cynical one that had Micah believing that she was about to snap.

"I can almost imagine how that conversation went. Myles's moral compass is so distorted. He probably threatened Ryan's life, and maybe even threw in a little blackmail."

She knew her brother well, Micah thought.

"Sadly, he also probably thought he was helping me or protecting me. Thought he was saving me from myself." She shook her head and then turned to Micah, her face a glowering mask of anger.

"So, I assume you showing up at the dance studio that day wasn't by chance. Were you there because Myles told you to be?"

"Not exactly," Micah hurried to say, not liking the direction her questions were going in. "I wanted to see you. Over the years, I've always asked him about you, wanting to know how you were doing and what you were up to."

"What you're saying is that you knew everything about me, even before that first dinner we had. You were just pretending to get to know me again. For what? So you could get close to me? So that you could make me fall in love with you all over again?" She threw the words at him as if throwing bricks, and they definitely hit their mark.

"It wasn't like that, Soul. My feelings for you are very real. Sure, our running into each other might've been staged, but everything that we've shared has been real."

The disappointment on her face and the hurt in her eyes would forever be burned in his mind. Maybe Myles had been right. Maybe it hadn't been a good idea to tell her anything, especially when Ryan might never contact her again.

"Myles was concerned that if Ryan came back into your life, that you'd believe whatever he told you. That you might end up as collateral damage if he made a misstep with the people he's working for. We didn't want you worrying about any of this since the situation might never touch you."

Her face reflected a barrage of emotions. Confusion. Hurt. Defeat. She paced the length of the small dining room deep in thought, and Micah wasn't sure what to expect next.

"Baby, you have to understand," he started but stopped when she glared at him.

"You didn't think I had sense enough to determine if someone had my best interest in mind? That I was so gullible that I would just take everything at face value? Myles has always been over the top, secretive and determined to take matters into his own hands, but you... How could you keep something like this from me? How could you pretend to care about me when you were just doing a job? You smiled in my face, made love to me like you really cared, but it was all some sick game."

"Hold up. *Wait!* It wasn't like that."

Micah's pulse raced, and he was afraid he was about to lose the best thing that ever happened to him. "Everything I said about my feelings for you was…*are* real. Baby, I love you. Should I have said something sooner about what was going on? Yes, I should've used better judgment and filled you in on what Myles was working on."

She put her hand on her forehead and huffed out a breath. "I am such a fool."

"No, you're not. I'm sorry if I hurt you, but don't *ever* think that I don't love you. That I'm not *in* love with you. You're it for me, sweetheart. And I'll do whatever it takes to make you believe that."

"I can't do this right now. I'm out of here."

Micah blocked her path. "Be mad at me all you want, but I want you safe."

"Right now, what you want doesn't matter to me. I've taken care of myself for years. I don't need you to take care of me. Use me for your own pleasure and then think you can dictate how I handle——"

"Just stop." He gripped her shoulders, keeping her from walking away. "If you hear from Ryan again, or if he shows up on your doorstep, you need to tell me, Myles, or call the police. He might be dangerous, Soul."

"Micah, he might've hurt my feelings by walking out on me, but he would never hurt me physically."

"You don't know that! He's involved with some dangerous people, and baby, we only want you safe. You have to believe that. Promise me that if you're ever in danger that you'll call me."

After a long hesitation, she nodded. Seeing the pain in her eyes was like taking a punch to the gut. Micah had vowed never to do anything to hurt her. Yet that's exactly what he'd done.

Lowering his forehead to hers, he breathed her in. "Even if you can't forgive me, please know that I love you. I swear I never meant to hurt you, and I'll do anything to make this right between us. Just tell me what to do." If going along with Myles's idea caused Micah to lose the love of his life, he was never going to forgive her brother.

Silently, Soul backed out of his hold and headed down the hall to the bedroom. Minutes later, she returned with her bag. "I think it's best that I leave," she said.

Micah nodded. He knew his conversation might drive her away. He'd give her a little space, but not too much.

"Let me grab my keys. I'll drive you home."

"That's not necessary. I already ordered an Uber."

"Come on, Soul. Don't leave like this. I know I should've said something sooner, but you know how I feel about you."

"I just need some time." She glanced at her phone. "My ride is here."

"At least let me carry your bag to the car."

She nodded and handed over the small suitcase. Following her out of the house, Micah tried to come up with the right words to get her to stay. He couldn't think of anything that hadn't already been said. He'd give her a couple of days and then try again.

After storing the suitcase in the trunk, he opened the back door for her. When she was settled inside, Micah leaned in and cupped her chin, forcing her to look at him. He was surprised she didn't pull away.

"Remember what I said. Any trouble, call me." She nodded again, and he did something that could easily get him slapped. He kissed her. He kissed her with everything in him, wanting her to feel how much he cared for her. "I love you. This...*we* aren't over."

Micah stood on the curb with his hands shoved into his pants pockets and watched the car pull away.

He meant what he said. This wasn't the end for them. He'd make sure of that.

Chapter Fifteen

*S*oul scrubbed the bathroom floor at the studio, trying to work out all of her pent-up energy. It had been almost a week since she'd seen Micah, but he was never far from her mind. Probably because he called every day, sometimes twice a day. He had told her once that he would call her daily for the rest of her life, whether she came back to him or not.

Soul smiled at the thought. Sure, she'd been angry at him and at her brother, but she knew them both well enough to know that they only had her best interest at heart. She just wished they weren't idiots. How could they have thought it a good idea to keep Ryan's activities from her? She could admit to finding everything about him hard to believe, but that didn't mean that she didn't think they could be true.

How in the world had he gotten involved with gun smugglers? That was something she would never know.

She also would never know if he had really loved her. But what did it matter? Her heart belonged to someone else.

"Soul?" Melissa called out.

"I'm back here." Soul stood and slid off the rubber gloves, then set them on the sink just as Melissa appeared in the doorway.

"I'm getting ready to leave. I put everything away in the main studio, but didn't get a chance to wipe down the mirrors."

"No problem. I'll take care of that. Thanks for your help tonight. I think the girls and their parents had a good time."

Melissa grinned. "Trust me, they did. Watching you and some of the people from your dance troupe perform was magical. I knew you were an amazing dancer, but to actually see you in action was beautiful."

Deep peace and satisfaction twirled inside of Soul. It felt good to perform again, even in front of a small group of people.

"Thank you," she said. "I'm just glad some of my friends were able to help me with the performance. I forgot how much fun it could be."

They talked for a few minutes longer until Soul's cell phone rang.

"Okay, that's my cue," Melissa said. "I'm going to change clothes before I leave. Have a good night."

"Thanks, you too," Soul said over her shoulder as she raced to her office, hoping to get to the phone before it stopped ringing.

"Hello," she said, a little out of breath. She dropped into her desk chair and swiveled back and forth.

"Hey, baby."

Soul's heart fluttered at the sound of Micah's deep voice. It didn't matter how often she heard from him. He still had the ability to make her body tingle. God, she missed him more than she cared to admit.

"Hi. How are you?" she asked.

"I'd be better if my woman wasn't still mad at me. You know it's been a week, right?"

"I know, but I needed that time to…" She needed the space to deal with her hurt feelings. It might've been childish, but Soul was still a little pissed at the situation, but not necessarily at him.

"You needed that time to what?"

She toyed with her dangling earring as she debated about how to respond. "I just needed time to think."

"And what did you come up with?"

She had come up with a lot of things, like how she loved Micah just as much now as she had years ago. But instead of saying that, she said, "I've missed you."

"I miss you too. Which is why I'm calling. I want to see you. Hold you. Grovel at your feet until you forgive me completely."

Soul laughed. "I actually like the sound of that, but can you also come bearing gifts?"

"Of course. What do you want? Flowers? Diamonds? A car? New leotards?

Soul burst out laughing, knowing that if he could,

he'd give her all of those things. "How about an extra-large order of fries? Uh, and you can throw in a diamond or two if you want."

Micah chuckled, and the deep richness of the sound warmed her heart. "You got it, baby. I'll see you soon."

After disconnecting, Soul held the phone to her chest. It had been hard staying mad at him. She had missed cuddling, kissing, and their intimate moments. As far as her brother was concerned, she was still a little ticked at him, and he knew it. The day after Micah had told her everything, she had called her brother and threatened to disown him if he ever interfered in her life again. Myles had blown off the threat and spewed a quick, *I love you, too.* Then he hung up on her.

Soul laughed at the memory and went back to work. Once she put her bathroom cleaning supplies away, she took the mirror cleaner into the biggest studio. If she hurried, she could shine the mirrors and then have time to change clothes before Micah arrived.

"Hello, Soul."

Soul screamed and spun around. Then she put her hand over her heart as if that could stop it from beating out of her chest. She hadn't heard anyone come in.

"Wha—what are you doing here?" she asked, shocked to see Ryan. He stood near the entrance of the room, appearing as nervous as she felt. Around six feet tall, medium build, and hair cut low, he still looked the same. Except he had lost ten or fifteen pounds, and the dark circles under his eyes made it seem as if he hadn't been sleeping. She guessed hiding from the Feds could do that to a person.

"I'm sorry I scared you, but I needed to see you. I needed to talk to you to explain what happened."

"That's not necessary, Ryan. I think you should go," she said, unable to hide the quiver in her voice.

Micah's words of warning about Ryan played inside her head. *He might be dangerous.* She'd like to think that he would never hurt her, but Soul didn't know him as well as she thought she had.

Instead of leaving, Ryan moved slowly into the large space, his eyes steady on her. Even though he didn't look intimidating, fear clawed through her body.

"I'm not going to hurt you. All I want to do is talk," he said as if reading her mind. Or maybe he saw fear on her face because on the inside, she was scared to death.

"It's been almost a year. I don't need an explanation. All I need is for you to leave. Please."

"I can't. Not until you hear me out. Not until you hear my side of the story."

Soul discretely glanced around the room looking for anything that could be used as a weapon. There was nothing except for the spray bottle that was light enough for her to pick up. As he moved closer, she eased away from him, looking for the perfect opportunity to get out of there.

"I assume your brother told you what happened, that he threatened me. He made me walk out on you. I didn't want to, but I had no choice."

"We always have a choice." Her voice cracked. "Instead, you walked away from me like I meant nothing to you." Soul knew how intimidating Myles could be, but she still didn't understand why Ryan couldn't have been honest with her. "If you had told me what Myles was up to, I could've talked to him. I could've helped you."

He shook his head wildly. "No. No, there was nothing you could've done. You don't know these people. They would've killed me if Myles had told them that I was a leak, or that I had stolen from them."

"You stole from them?" she asked before she could stop herself.

Ryan hesitated before saying no, and Soul knew he was lying. He had a tell. Whenever he was lying, he tugged on his right earlobe. She had noticed it early in their relationship, but it hadn't been a big deal. The few times that she had caught him lying were times when he didn't want to hurt her feelings. Like when she'd made lasagna and asked if he liked it. Or when she had dyed her hair red, and it hadn't turned out very well.

"Ryan, I don't need to hear anymore. Please, just go." She kept moving, but each step she took in one direction, hoping she could get past him, he moved too.

"Not until you let me tell you everything. And I need you to stop moving!"

Soul froze. Panic twisted inside of her.

He lifted his hands out in front of him. "Listen, I'm sorry I yelled. I just…this is hard for me. I need you to understand that I didn't know who Ebolsa was."

"Ho—how did you get wrapped up with someone who smuggles guns?"

"I didn't know. Ebolsa hired me years ago to be his accountant. For the first two years, it was just a normal client relationship. Then he started wanting me to make deposits to a lot of different accounts, and I got suspicious. Then it was other little things that built into big situations."

"You were in business with him before you met me. Why would you risk my life like that?"

"I didn't mean to, but you were so nice to me. After we started hanging out, I fell in love with you. I didn't want to lose you."

"You couldn't have loved me. Otherwise, you wouldn't have put me in danger."

"I didn't mean to."

He ran a nervous hand over his head and Soul could tell he was getting agitated. She inched to the side, little by little, hoping he wouldn't notice her moving. She only had one shot at getting out of there.

"I love you, Soul. I'm leaving the country, and I want you to go with me."

She looked at him like he was crazy. "I'm not going anywhere with you."

"Don't say that. Don't—"

Soul snatched up the spray bottle and shot it, then darted past him, barely escaping his clutches when he reached for her. Fear clawed through her veins as she ran out of the room. She made it to the hallway before stumbling and screamed when he grabbed her foot, sending her crashing to the floor.

"Soul, stop. I'm not going to hurt you!"

"Then let me go!" she shouted, not taking any chances. If he weren't going to hurt her, he would've backed away. She kept kicking until she kicked him in the mouth. That sent him falling back, howling in pain.

She got up and ran to her office for her cell phone. Before she could lock the door, Ryan burst in and lifted her off her feet.

"Let me go!" she wiggled in his grasp, kicking, screaming, and scratching his face.

"Stop. I'm not trying to hurt you. I need you to go with me!" he yelled, but he wouldn't let her go. His arms were tight around her waist.

"Help!" she screamed over and over again, pounding against his chest.

"Let her go!" Micah roared, seeming to come out of nowhere. When he grabbed Ryan from behind, Soul tumbled to the floor. She cried out when she landed on her hip bone but managed to slide out of the way.

Micah threw Ryan up against the wall, then wrestled him to the ground. He punched him over and over until Ryan stopped moving.

"Is he…is he dead?"

Breathing hard, Micah staggered to his feet. "No," he said and reached for her. Pulling her roughly into his arms, he held her tightly. "God, baby. Are you okay? Did he hurt you?" His concerned gaze traveled over her.

"I...I'll be fine." Her body ached, but that was nothing considering the alternative.

Without releasing her, Micah pulled his cell phone from his pocket. "I need to call this in."

MICAH DEALT WITH CRIMINALS EVERY DAY, BUT HE couldn't ever remember being as afraid as he'd been earlier. On his way to the dance studio, Myles had called him to tell him that his contact had lost track of Ryan. Micah freaked. Especially when he called Soul to give her a heads-up, and she didn't answer.

But nothing could've prepared him for arriving at her place and hearing her earth-shattering screams. Even now, as they sat cuddled together on his sofa, he didn't even want to think about what might've happened if he hadn't arrived when he had.

Ryan had been arrested and would be transferred into federal custody. Micah wasn't sure what would happen at this point. Chances were, the Feds would keep him in protective custody and offer him a deal if he testified against Ebolsa.

"Do you want some of these?" Soul asked, holding up the container of French fries.

"Nah, baby. I'm good. Are you sure that's going to be enough for you, though? Do you want anything else?"

She leaned her head back, which put her mouth in the perfect position for him to kiss her sweet lips, and he did. Since they arrived at his place, Micah hadn't been able to stop kissing her and holding her. He could've lost her today, and that thought shook him to the core.

"I need you to scoot over for a minute," he said when the kiss ended.

Standing up, he strolled into the dining room to the jacket he had hanging on the back of one of the chairs. He dug through the pockets until he found what he was looking for.

Soul watched him as he walked back into the room. She moved over so he could reclaim his seat, but instead, he dropped down on one knee.

Her eyes grew round. "Uh, what are you doing?"

"Something I wanted to do years ago. I love you, Soul. I fell in love with you the first time we met in that pizza joint. I messed up my chance with you last time, but if you marry me, I promise I'll never let you go again. I will love you until I take my last breath. Will you marry me?"

He opened the black velvet box that held a two-carat diamond ring, which he had purchased the day after their big argument.

Soul squealed and threw her arms around his neck. "Yes! Yes, I'll marry you!"

Epilogue

leven months later...

WHO SAYS DREAMS DON'T COME TRUE?

"She's beautiful," Soul whispered, as she cradled her baby girl. Awed by the miracle of being able to bring a life into the world, all she could do was stare at the precious jewel in her arms. Mikera was only four hours old, and already Soul was hopelessly in love.

"Scoot over." Micah climbed onto the hospital bed and gathered Soul into his arms as she held their daughter. "She's perfect," he said, brushing the back of his finger down the baby's soft cheek. "She's absolutely perfect, just like her mommy. Thank you for this remarkable gift."

Soul tilted her head just enough to kiss her supersexy, amazing husband. The last eleven months had been a whirlwind, and Micah had become her world; a world she couldn't imagine living in without him. They'd had a small church wedding a month after he proposed. She had thought that was a little quick until he'd said, *why wait?*

After they returned from their Hawaii honeymoon, another major decision had taken place. Micah left the police department and started working for Supreme Security. He was officially one of *Atlanta's Finest*, in more ways than one. The money was better. The hours were flexible. And the work, providing personal security to the rich and famous, was safer than patrolling the streets of Atlanta.

Soul's dance studio was thriving. All of their classes were full, and they had a waiting list, something she never imagined happening. She had hired three more instructors, as well as a company to clean the building. After the run-in with Ryan while she'd been alone in the studio, Micah had insisted that there always be at least two people there at any given time. Which was okay with Soul. She didn't worry about seeing Ryan again since he was now in witness protection. And she rested easy, knowing that Ebolsa was behind bars.

Now she and Micah were living their most dramatic change of all. They were parents.

Soul glanced down at their sleeping beauty, still trying to wrap her brain around the fact that she was a mommy. Micah had been there for her through every minute of the fifteen-hour labor, never wavering with his encouragement and support. She felt so blessed. Not a day went by that she didn't thank God for bringing him back into her life.

Despite her initial fear of having a child, she and Micah had started trying immediately after they were married. And though Soul had been thrilled when they found out she was pregnant, that fear that had been a constant companion much of her adult life crept back in. She wanted a baby but didn't want to suffer the same fate as her mother. She wanted to live to see her child grow up. Though Micah didn't know for sure what would happen, he had insisted that she would be fine, that their baby would be fine. He said it often enough until Soul believed him.

"Did your mom leave?" she asked as he repositioned himself on the bed, looking more comfortable.

"Yeah, she'll be back a little later. Do you know she's already talking about us having another baby?"

Soul laughed. "I'm not surprised. The other day, after I told her that me having six kids was out of the question, she negotiated me down to three."

Micah wiggled his brows and grinned at her. "Just say when, and I'll be happy to do my part."

"Yeah, I'm sure you will."

Silence fell between them as they stared down at Mikera.

"We did it," Micah said, suddenly sounding as tired as she felt. "We really did it."

She smiled at him. "Yes, we did, and I'm happier than I ever thought I could be."

"And if you're happy, I'm happy."

Micah leaned down and kissed her with so much love that Soul thought her heart would burst. She was a witness that dreams really did come true. The life they were building together was everything Soul desired.

If you enjoyed this book by Sharon C. Cooper,
Please consider leaving a review on Amazon, review site or social media outlet.

Don't forget to grab the other books in the Unparalleled Love Series!

EVERLASTING DESIRE BY STEPHANIE NICOLE NORRIS - HTTPS://AMZN.TO/2ZJLSSR

Discovering the truth behind her boyfriend's infidelity, Jada Wilson decides it's time to regain her independence. She wants to shed her anxiety, and while looking for a stress-free resolution, the answer to her quandary comes from an unanticipated source—her best friend. He's been the only consistent person in her life, and the unexpected way his touch ignites a passion within her takes Jada to new heights she wasn't ready to explore, until now.

AWARD-WINNING MASTERCHEF SOLOMON MCBRIDE HAS reached the end of his reservations regarding Jada Wilson. As her best friend for the past three decades, Solomon's had enough of witnessing her heart break. But aware of her vulnerability, he carefully treads a path to rebuild her trust in love, and he's ready to lead the way if she is willing to allow him.

HEART'S DESIRE BY DELANEY DIAMOND - https://amzn.to/2Z6E3H9

Co-workers Nathan Crenshaw and Janice Livingston once had a passionate relationship that went up in flames and created a strained environment at their place of employment. Since then Janice has tried to move on. Unfortunately, they have to work together, and unfortunately, she's still very attracted to Nathan.

NATHAN CAN'T FORGET HIS CONNECTION WITH JANICE—A connection he hasn't experienced with any other woman. After an earth-shattering kiss rekindles their flame, will these two finally get it right—or will an outside force get in the way?

Join Sharon's Mailing List

To get sneak peeks of upcoming stories and to hear about
giveaways that Sharon is sponsoring,

join her mailing list at https://sharoncooper.net/newsletter.

About the Author

Award-winning and bestselling author, Sharon C. Cooper, is a romance-a-holic - loving anything that involves romance with a happily-ever-after, whether in books, movies, or real life. Sharon writes contemporary romance, as well as romantic suspense and enjoys rainy days, carpet picnics, and peanut butter and jelly sandwiches. She's been nominated for numerous awards and is the recipient of Emma Awards (RSJ) for Author of the Year 2019, Favorite Hero 2019 (INDEBTED), Romantic Suspense of the Year 2015 (TRUTH OR CONSEQUENCES), Interracial Romance of the Year 2015 (ALL YOU'LL EVER NEED), and BRAB (book club) Award -Breakout Author of the Year 2014. When Sharon isn't writing, she's hanging out with her amazing husband, doing volunteer work or reading a good book (a romance of course). To read more about Sharon and her novels, visit www.sharoncooper.net

Website: https://sharoncooper.net
Join Sharon's mailing list: https://bit.ly/31Xsm36

Facebook fan page: http://www.facebook.com/AuthorSharonCCooper21?ref=hl

Twitter: https://twitter.com/#!/Sharon_Cooper1

Subscribe to her blog: http://sharonccooper.wordpress.com/

Goodreads: http://www.goodreads.com/author/show/5823574.Sharon_C_Cooper

Pinterest: https://www.pinterest.com/sharonccooper/

Instagram: https://www.instagram.com/authorsharonccooper/

Other Titles

Atlanta's Finest Series
A Passionate Kiss (book 1- prequel)
Vindicated (book 2)
Indebted (book 3)
Accused (book 4)
Betrayed (book 5) – coming soon
Hunted (book 6) – coming soon

Jenkins & Sons Construction Series (Contemporary Romance)
Love Under Contract (book 1)
Proposal for Love (book 2)
A Lesson on Love (book 3)
Unplanned Love (book 4)

Jenkins Family Series (Contemporary Romance)
Best Woman for the Job (Short Story Prequel)
Still the Best Woman for the Job (book 1)
All You'll Ever Need (book 2)
Tempting the Artist (book 3)
Negotiating for Love (book 4)
Seducing the Boss Lady (book 5)
Love at Last (Holiday Novella)
When Love Calls (Novella)

Reunited Series (Romantic Suspense)
Blue Roses (book 1)
Secret Rendezvous (Prequel to Rendezvous with Danger)
Rendezvous with Danger (book 2)
Truth or Consequences (book 3)
Operation Midnight (book 4)

Stand Alones
Something New ("Edgy" Sweet Romance)
Legal Seduction (Harlequin Kimani – Contemporary
Romance)
Sin City Temptation (Harlequin Kimani –
Contemporary Romance)
A Dose of Passion (Harlequin Kimani – Contemporary
Romance)
Model Attraction (Harlequin Kimani – Contemporary
Romance)